"The preliminary tests are back," the elderly doctor said, his penetrating brown eyes grave with concern. "The tests point to cancer, specifically, acute lymphocytic leukemia. It's one of the most common forms of cancer among kids. A bone marrow aspiration will confirm the preliminary diagnosis." His voice sounded concerned, but final.

A kid! That's what I am, Dawn thought. She *was* a kid, just two months over her thirteenth birthday. . . .

"Are you going to be my doctor?" she asked, her voice trembling. *Don't cry!* she pleaded to herself. *Please don't start crying, Dawn. Don't be a baby!*

SIX MONTHS TO LIVE

Lurlene McDaniel

SCHOLASTIC INC.

New York Toronto London Auckland Sydney
Mexico City New Delhi Hong Kong Buenos Aires

This book is lovingly dedicated to Rochelle Lynn Dove and her family.

I would like to thank Joan Bompane for her helpful input and all the dedicated health personnel who are warring with childhood cancer.

Cover photo and design
by Michael Petty
Petty Productions

ISBN 0-439-69213-X

12 11 10 9 8 7 6 5 4 3 2   4 5 6 7 8 9/0

Printed in the U.S.A.   01

First Scholastic printing, September 2004

CHAPTER
1

When Dawn Rochelle was thirteen years old, they told her she had cancer. She sat in her doctor's office, clutching her mother's hand who sat clutching her father's hand and stared at the familiar face of Dr. Galland with disbelief.

"H-How can this be?" her mother asked.

"We thought it was just the flu," her father gasped.

Dawn said nothing. She couldn't think clearly, much less talk. Yet, the look on Dr. Galland's face told them that he was *not* joking. The look on his tanned, lined face told them that he was deadly serious.

"The preliminary tests are back," the elderly doctor said, his penetrating brown eyes grave with concern. "The tests point to cancer, specifically, acute lymphocytic leukemia. It's one of the most common forms of cancer among kids. A bone marrow aspiration will confirm the preliminary diagnosis." His voice sounded concerned, but final.

A kid! That's what I am, Dawn thought. She *was* a kid, just two months over her thirteenth birthday . . . a seventh grader . . . cheerleader for Adams Junior High . . . daughter of Pete and Meggie Rochelle . . . kid sister of 18-year-old Rob Rochelle . . . super fan of Michael Jackson . . . collector of teddy bears . . . a resident of Columbus, Ohio . . . and now, a victim of cancer.

"Are you going to be my doctor?" she asked, her voice trembling. *Don't cry!* she pleaded to herself. *Please don't start crying, Dawn. Don't be a baby!*

Dr. Galland shook his head. He reached forward and took her free hand in his. Looking deep into her green eyes he said, "I've treated you since you were born, Dawn. I've seen you through the chicken pox, lots of colds and flus, some ear infections and even a broken arm."

She nodded, remembering their medical history together. "But," he continued, "you need specialists for this, Dawn . . . doctors who only treat kids with cancer . . . doctors who will be able to help you fight off this disease with modern weapons." He paused, sensing her distress. "But I will come visit you regularly at Children's Hospital."

"Hospital?" Dawn gasped. Bewildered, she looked at her parents. "I've got to go to the hospital? I-I don't want to!" she protested.

Her father intervened. "Dr. Galland, this

diagnosis is hard to accept," he said. His tone sounded angry. "How can you be sure? I mean, a week ago we brought Dawn in for a checkup because she was tired all the time. And now you say, 'Cancer.' We want a second opinion."

Her mother agreed. Dawn felt sorry for her parents. They looked so scared.

"I sent a blood sample to the lab when she was here," Dr. Galland told them. "I suspected it then. Her symptoms were classic ... chronic sore throat, swollen glands, weakness and constant fatigue ... coupled with the unexplained bruises on her arms and legs, and bleeding without clotting. At the hospital, they will do the bone marrow aspiration test I mentioned. That will confirm the diagnosis."

Dawn looked down self-consciously at her legs. The huge, angry-looking bruises glared back at her. They had been a road sign to Dr. Galland, a road sign that had said: "Cancer." She had thought she was getting them at cheer-leading practice.

"Those same symptoms could just be the flu," Pete Rochelle snapped.

"It isn't the flu," Dr. Galland said quietly.

The late April afternoon sun came through the blinds in his tan and burgundy-colored office making straight, flat, horizontal lines across his shoulders and the surface of his desk. The glaring light hurt Dawn's eyes. "How long?" she asked, trying to accept a stay in the hospital.

"You will need to stay until you get on a medication program that sends you into remission," Dr. Galland said.

"Remission?" she asked.

"The state of keeping the cancer cells from spreading . . . and making your symptoms disappear," he defined.

"How soon?" she wondered, blinking hard.

"This afternoon," he told her gently.

Dawn sat bolt upright. "T-Today?" she asked.

"As soon as possible," he confirmed.

"But . . . but I have school tomorrow. And I have cheerleading practice after school. And a term paper's due . . . ."

"I've already made arrangements with the Oncology floor at Children's Hospital," Dr. Galland told her tenderly. "The sooner, the better, Dawn. The sooner we begin fighting this invader, the better your chances of recovery."

Dawn's knuckles were white from holding her mother's hand so tightly. But she didn't let go. If she did, she was afraid she might start crying. And she didn't want to cry, not here in front of Dr. Galland.

"What do you want us to do?" Mrs. Rochelle asked. Her voice sounded trembly to Dawn's ears.

"Go home, pack some things for Dawn . . . personal items, no valuables," Dr. Galland explained. "At the hospital, after you get checked in, they'll take you up to the floor. The

8

nurses will help get Dawn settled. They're expecting you."

They're expecting me! Dawn thought. Just like that. They were expecting her on the Oncology floor of the hospital to begin treatment of her cancer. Dawn swallowed the fear that had risen in her mouth.

"I-I . . . Will I get well . . ?" she asked, timidly, unable to focus on the alternatives.

Dr. Galland looked at her fondly. "They've made great strides in leukemia research," he said. "The best, most modern and finest medical technology will be yours."

His words should have comforted her. But they did not. They only made her feel small and scared and anxious – medical research. Suddenly, she felt like a white rat trapped in a science experiment . . . caught in a maze of mind-boggling proportions . . . a maze with no exit . . . a rat with no future.

* * * * *

"It can't be true. I want another opinion, Meggie," Dawn's father said as he paced restlessly around the floor of Dawn's green and yellow bedroom. Dawn watched him pace. His white shirt sleeves were rolled up. His tie was loosened around his neck.

"We'll get lots of opinions at the hospital, Pete," Dawn's mother said as she mechanically packed her daughter's suitcase.

Dawn sat on the bed. Her arms clutched around her knees, pulled tightly against her chest. She barely heard her parent's conversation. She felt numb all over.

What will I tell my friends? she wondered. How would she tell them something like this? *Hi, Kim and Kathy and Jill and Rhonda. This is Dawn. Remember me? Remember how I said I had to go for a checkup today? Well, guess what? I have cancer.*

How would she tell her teachers? *Gee, Mr. Collins. Sorry about that term paper. But I have cancer, you know.*

What would she say to her grandparents? *Sorry, I can't come visit you this summer. But I'll be in the hospital. I have cancer.*

Dawn looked all around her bedroom. A soft breeze ruffled the curtains back and the sun streamed in the window. Her desk was cluttered with piles of papers, a notebook and books that were ragged from nearly a year of school and studies.

A menagerie of teddy bears grinned down at her from bookshelves and a glass curio case. There were big bears and tiny bears of all colors. There were bears with pot bellies, bears with flat bellies. Some bears had hearts or rainbows sewn on their fronts. Dawn had been collecting them since she was two. The last time she'd counted them she counted 103 teddy bears.

Mr. Ruggers, her very first and very favorite bear, peered at her through his one good eye. She wanted to tell him, "I have cancer, Mr. Ruggers. What am I going to do?" Instead, she said, "If people want to come see me in the hospital, please tell them not to give me any stupid teddy bears."

Mrs. Rochelle stopped packing and dropped onto the bed next to her daughter. She put her arm around Dawn's shoulders. "Oh, Baby. I wish this was happening to me instead of you," she said.

Dawn shrugged, trying to shake off her mother's arm. "Well, it's not," she said irritably.

"Honey," her father said, reaching out and touching her. "We'll get the best doctors there are."

She shrugged him off, too. "So what?" she asked. "What can the doctors do about it? Can they make it go away? Will they make me well again?"

Neither one of her parents could answer her. Dawn looked at both of them. Their faces looked so grim. She knew they were terrific parents. They couldn't help what had happened to her. She shouldn't treat them meanly. "Sorry," she mumbled meekly.

"I'll call Rob tonight," her mom said.

Rob . . . Dawn pictured her brother. He was so big and broad across his shoulders. He'd gotten a football scholarship to Michigan State last fall.

11

Big, brotherly Rob was the one who used to tease and torment her. He called her "Squirt" and tickled her until tears ran down her cheeks. Rob used to hide her tennis shoes and rearrange her teddy bears and take her to the movies and skating and . . .

"There's nothing he can do," Dawn said testily.

"He'll want to know," her father said.

Her mother snapped the catches on Dawn's suitcase. "All done," she said.

"What if we forgot something?" Dawn asked hastily. Suddenly she dreaded leaving the safety and familiarity of her bedroom.

"I'll bring it by later," her mom said.

"But what about school?" she asked. "No one knows . . ." She felt panic rise in her. *The hospital!* she thought. *What will they do to me? How many shots will they give me? What's going to happen to me?*

Her dad sat down and put his arm around her small frame. "It's all right to cry, you know," he said.

Dawn blinked very hard and angrily forced down the rising lump in her throat. "I'm not going to cry!" she told him through gritted teeth. "It won't help. It won't change anything!"

Mr. Rochelle hugged his daughter to him. Then he took Dawn's hand and stood up, tugging her gently to her feet. They started toward the door of her bedroom. Dawn couldn't remember

12

the last time her dad had taken her hand and led her. Maybe it happened when she was four, when she was crossing the street, or helping her up after she'd fallen off her bike.

He looped her arm through his and patted her hand. "We love you, Dawn," he said softly. "And we'll be there for you, no matter what."

Dawn believed her father and offered him a small smile. She took one long last look around her bedroom, avoiding the one-eyed stare of Mr. Ruggers. Then she followed her parents out the door.

CHAPTER
2

Dawn surveyed the room at the hospital with fear and wonder. It was a cheerful yellow room with a window dressed in crisp white and yellow checks. Yet the room scared her, too. The hospital bed looked like a small prison with the bedrails raised. The bone marrow aspiration test had been scary, but it was over. Now Dawn's interest was focused on the preparations for her upcoming hospital stay.

A nurse, Fredia, chattered gaily as she bustled about the room. She pulled back the curtain partition that revealed a second bed. Although there was no one in the other bed, it was obvious that it had been occupied.

"Your roomie is a real doll," Nurse Fredia bubbled to Dawn and her parents. "Her name is Sandy Chandler. She's 13 years old and she's from West Virginia. Like you, she's newly diagnosed with lymphocytic leukemia. She's only been here a couple of weeks, but everybody on the floor really likes her."

Dawn wasn't crazy about the news. She didn't want a roommate. She wanted to be alone.

"Dr. Sinclair and his team will be in soon to talk to you and your family and explain the treatment you'll begin. I'm on the day shift, Dawn. If you want anything, please ask me." The older woman smiled at the young girl. Dawn responded by smiling back. Nurse Fredia was so friendly that Dawn couldn't help but like her.

True to Nurse Fredia's prediction, Dr. Sinclair and two white-coated doctors entered the room. Dr. Sinclair was a tall man with thick, blond hair, blue eyes and a moustache. After a round of self-conscious introductions, Dr. Sinclair settled Dawn and her family into chairs and began to talk to them.

"First," he emphasized, "I want you all to know that we level with our patients and their families one hundred percent. We tell you the truth. We don't hide any facts from you. We answer your questions as honestly as we can. Understand?"

The Rochelles nodded in unison. "All right," he continued. "Let me tell you what's going to happen. Leukemia is a disease of the parts of the body that make blood. For unknown reasons, the body starts making abnormal white blood cells. This means that production of red cells decreases. That's why you're anemic, Dawn. That's why you feel tired all the time."

Dawn nodded. She *had* felt very tired and weak. "The disease also effects the platelets in your blood which cause clotting and keep a

16

person from bleeding to death every time he cuts himself. Do you have trouble stopping small wounds from bleeding?" Dr. Sinclair asked.

"Yes," Dawn told him. "Whenever I brush my teeth, my gums bleed for no reason. And . . . and I have to be extra careful when I shave my legs. One cut bleeds and bleeds," she added shyly.

He confirmed her words with a nod of his head. "Red blood is produced in your bone marrow. Leukemia disrupts that production. These maverick white blood cells invade the bone marrow and cause havoc. The result is swollen lymph nodes, spleen, liver and kidneys."

"What are you going to do?" Dawn asked, awed by the idea of her own body turning against itself.

"The first line of defense in this kind of leukemia is chemotherapy," Dr. Sinclair said. He leaned against the window sill and crossed his arms over his chest.

"We're going to begin giving you some very powerful drugs to kill the abnormal cells, or at least slow their growth," Dr. Sinclair said. He smiled and Dawn noticed his straight, white teeth. "In fifty to ninety percent of all cases we achieve remission so that you can go home, go back to school and resume a normal life."

Go home! Dawn thought. The idea almost caused tears to come to her eyes.

"The other kind of chemotherapy has a long name. But it means that you'll get a powerful

17

combination of various drugs intravenously," he said.

Dawn swallowed. Needles! They were going to stick her full of needles and let stuff drip into her veins. She shuddered. "Is that why I have to stay in the hospital?" she asked.

"Yes," Dr. Sinclair answered.

"How long?" she asked, wide-eyed.

"Until we achieve remission," he said kindly. "It can take weeks or months. We administer the drugs in rounds, trying different combinations until we find what's right for you. You'll be on one week and off one week," he further explained. "We try and get you out of here as quickly as possible. Since you live in the city, you can come back as an outpatient for monitoring. Your roommate, Sandy, is from a rural area. So she'll stay here for as long as necessary to achieve remission. It isn't feasible for her to be an outpatient."

"Will I always have to take the drugs? I mean, even after I go home?" Dawn asked.

"Yes," he said. "That's called maintenance therapy. It usually lasts two to three years."

Stunned, Dawn blurted, "Won't I ever get well?"

"If you remain in remission for five years, we consider you cured," the doctor said, smiling.

"Dr. Sinclair," Dawn's mom asked quietly. "What if we decide to skip all this therapy and just take Dawn home?"

The blue-eyed doctor surveyed her and said, "That would be very unwise, Mrs. Rochelle. Untreated, ninety percent of all leukemia victims die within a year."

Dead! A kind of relief flooded through Dawn at the sound of the word. At last, someone had finally said it . . . *Dead*. All day everyone had avoided the word. Leukemia kills, Dawn realized. "I-I don't want to die," she mumbled softly.

"That's why you're here," Dr. Sinclair said, "so that you can live. The next several weeks will be tough. The drugs will make you very sick. You may lose your hair. You'll definitely lose your appetite. You'll be poked and stuck and you'll feel sad and angry at all of us. But in the end, you'll go into remission and your chances are really good that you will survive." His eyes looked determined and Dawn realized something as she looked into them.

Dr. Sinclair hated leukemia. Like a person hates evil, he hated the disease. It comforted her to know that he was on her side. He was going to help her fight this terrible war that was going on within her body.

After Dr. Sinclair and his assistants left, Dawn changed into a hospital gown. She unpacked the small collection of items she'd brought from home. She filled the bedside table with perfumed soap, toothbrush and toothpaste, deodorant and some makeup supplies. She went into the adjoining bathroom and surveyed her face in the mirror.

It was a pleasant face, not beautiful, but cute with the Rochelle family nose and her mother's clear green eyes. She brushed her long, auburn hair and tied it up in a pony tail. "So," she told her reflection, "in a few weeks I may be bald." It bothered her a lot. It had taken her years to grow her hair past her shoulders. "I'll get it cut tomorrow!" she said firmly. If she was going to be bald, then she'd get used to short hair right now!

Her dinner tray arrived and her parents went down to the hospital cafeteria for their dinner. The food was tasty, but Dawn didn't have much of an appetite. Absently, she wondered when her fabled roommate was going to appear. But Dawn ate all her dinner alone with no trace of Sandy Chandler.

A lab technician entered rattling a tray of bottles, tubes and syringes. Dawn felt her heart skip. She was going to be stuck with needles. Dawn's suspicions were confirmed. The technician rolled up Dawn's sleeve and encircled her arm with a thick rubber band.

The woman talked cheerfully as she poked around for Dawn's vein. When she found the vein, she slid the long syringe into it. Fascinated, Dawn watched the attached tube fill with her blood. Next, the lab technician stuck another needle into a vein on Dawn's forearm. Then she slipped a thin, clear tube into the vein, attached a permanent vial, clamped it off and taped the entire contraption down. Oddly, it didn't hurt.

"I'm doing this so we don't have to stick you every time we need a blood sample," the technician explained, sensing Dawn's questions. "Now, I'll be able to undo the clamp, drain out the blood sample and close it up again without sticking you. The clamp acts like a floodgate."

Once she'd left, Dawn stared at the attached tube. *Vampires!* she thought. The place seemed full of vampires.

Her parents returned from supper and stood awkwardly in the room. "You can go home," Dawn told them. "I-I'll just watch some T.V."

They both looked tired and strained. "I'll be back first thing in the morning," her mom said.

"I'll stop off on my way to the office," her father added.

"Do you want me to call some of your friends?" her mother asked. "Or do you want to?" She eyed the telephone next to Dawn's bed.

"You can," Dawn said. They'd find out sooner or later. But she wasn't up to telling anybody just yet.

Her parents kissed her good night and left. Dawn lay in the unfamiliar bed blinking back a sudden rush of helpless tears. "Stop it!" she commanded herself. "Crying won't help!"

Nurse Fredia entered the room. "Here it is,"

she announced, setting down a small silver tray full of paper cups. Each cup was filled with some kind of medication. She handed Dawn three of them. "This is your first round of chemotherapy," she explained. "Here are two capsules, a clear liquid and a red liquid."

Hesitantly, Dawn swallowed the offered contents. She wrinkled her nose and said, "Ugh! That one tastes awful."

Nurse Fredia smiled and straightened the covers around Dawn's small form. "Just think about all the good they'll do for you. Think of them as allies," she said.

But before Dawn could say anything else, an orderly wheeled a stretcher bed into the room. The pale, still form of a young girl lay on the gurney.

"Hi, Sandy!" Nurse Fredia greeted, ignoring the girl's inability to react. "This is your roommate, Dawn Rochelle. You two are going to be great friends! I just know it."

Sandy tried to roll her eyes toward Dawn, but she seemed too weak, too sick to manage a greeting. Dawn's heart ached for her. She watched as the orderly's strong arms lifted Sandy from the gurney into her bed. Sandy moaned weakly. Nurse Fredia tucked her in and offered her a sip of water.

For a minute Dawn thought that Sandy might throw up. But she didn't. "Sandy just took IV chemotherapy," Fredia explained. "She'll be all right in a few hours."

Dawn stared at the frail, ill-looking Sandy. She was a cute girl, very blonde, with a tipped-up nose and a smathering of freckles sprinkled across it. *Is this going to happen to me?* Dawn thought in a panic.

"I'm going off duty now," Nurse Fredia told Dawn. "The night nurse is Gail. Please ring for her if either of you want anything."

Dawn agreed, numbly. Everything was so businesslike! Sandy looked so pale and sick, and yet things went on at the hospital like nothing was different. Again, Dawn felt tears of frustration rise to her eyes. *I won't cry!* she reminded herself, fiercely.

That night, Dawn lay alone in the dark, unable to sleep for a long time. When Nurse Gail came in to check her at midnight, Dawn asked, "How's Sandy?"

"Still awake?" Nurse Gail asked, surprised.

"I-I was just wondering about Sandy," Dawn said.

"She's sleeping," Nurse Gail told Dawn. She bent over to fluff Dawn's pillow slightly.

"I-I took my medicine tonight," Dawn said. "And I'm not . . . I don't feel sick," she said hopefully.

Gail smiled down at her tenderly. "I'd love to tell you that you won't be sick," she said quietly, patting her shoulder. "But almost everyone reacts that way. I'm sorry, but that's the truth."

CHAPTER
3

Waves of nausea washed over Dawn in the bright, warm light of the new morning. She struggled to sit up, unable to think about anything but the queasiness in her stomach. Nurse Gail's prediction had proven true. The medicine had made Dawn sick. She still had more medication to take this morning!

"Hi!" the voice called from the bed next to her. Dawn momentarily forgot her discomfort. She turned to see the wan, but smiling face of Sandy.

"Hi," Dawn answered weakly.

"It'll pass," the cute blonde-haired girl assured her, understanding Dawn's feelings. "It did for me." For the first time, Dawn noticed Sandy's soft, lilting West Virginian accent. "You've just got to think about something pleasant. Besides, they'll be bringin' in the breakfast trays soon."

Dawn moaned as renewed nausea swept over her. "Don't say 'food' to me," she mumbled.

"Oh, but you'd better eat," Sandy warned. "If not, they'll hook you up to IVs. Sit up straight and take some deep breaths," Sandy urged. "You'll feel a lot better."

The thought of more needles dripping stuff into her body helped Dawn swallow the bad taste in her mouth. She sat up straighter and followed Sandy's instruction. It helped.

"Sorry I was such poor company last night," Sandy drawled. She gave Dawn a sweet smile and Dawn smiled back.

"You didn't look very well," Dawn confessed.

"I know. The first time, my daddy got so upset that he almost took me out of the hospital that night!" Sandy said. She gave a smile of remembrance and said, "My daddy's like that. Can't stand anythin' hurtin' his little girl."

Dawn giggled. "My father's like that, too."

"I'm glad to have a roommate," Sandy told her. "It gets awfully lonesome around here. My folks had to go back home. They both work and they only come up on weekends."

Dawn felt ashamed of her previous thoughts about having a roommate and knew that she was going to like Sandy a lot. She seemed so sweet and friendly. And Dawn thought Sandy's accent was cute.

Sandy chattered over breakfast telling Dawn about her hometown in West Virginia. She told about her two brothers and younger sister, and about her school and assorted friends. "At first when they told me I had cancer, I just didn't believe them!" Sandy said.

"And my Pa . . . well, he about hit the roof. Then he got all involved and decided I'd have the 'best treatment available,' " Sandy mimicked her father's gruff, booming voice.

Dawn laughed. "So . . . here I am," Sandy finished brightly. "I've just been here two weeks, but they tell me I'm doin' real well."

Another round of medication followed Dawn's morning meal and then both girls took turns bathing and putting on their makeup. Dawn discovered that Sandy was Barbie-doll cute. Her cheeks glowed with pale pink blusher. Her straight white-blonde hair was pulled back with brightly colored combs and hung down her back. Dawn had second thoughts about getting her own long red-brown hair cut.

Dawn introduced Sandy to her dad when he stopped by and again to her mom when she arrived. "Your father and I talked to Rob last night," Dawn's mother said. "He was pretty upset. He says he'll be home this weekend."

"Gosh, Mom, he doesn't have to . . ." Dawn started.

"He *wants* to see you, Dawn." Her mom paused. "I also talked to our minister. The whole congregation will start praying for you," she said, her eyes shining. "People have been so kind, Dawn. They're all rooting for you. Oh, I called Kim and Rhonda. Both of them started crying

27

and said they'll come see you tonight during visiting hours. I'm going to visit your school principal this afternoon. You'll have to finish your school work in the hospital so you can at least stay up with your class."

Dawn nodded, half dreading the visit from her friends. What would she say to them? How would they treat her? What would they think? She didn't want to answer a bunch of dumb questions!

Dawn, her mom and Sandy played a few hands of cards. Shortly after her mom left, Dawn started feeling sick to her stomach and had to return to her bed. After lunch, another white-coated doctor arrived.

"Hello, Dawn . . . Sandy." The slim woman with brown hair and brown eyes greeted them as she breezed into their room. "I'm Bonnie Knee-land. I'm a doctor, a psychotherapist," she said.

A shrink! Dawn thought. *I'm not crazy. I don't need a head doctor!*

"My specialty is helping kids with cancer help in their own healing process," Dr. Kneeland told them. She pulled up a chair and settled between the two beds, smoothing the front of her red linen skirt with her hands. She continued confidently, "It's my job to help you fight back. Sometimes, the hardest part of treating cancer is getting the patient involved with her own treatment.

"We know how helpless you patients feel," Dr.

Kneeland said. "All we doctors do is poke you, examine you and test you." Dawn nodded. She already felt that way, and she hadn't even been there 24 hours!

"Well, I want to help you help yourselves. Tell me, Dawn, when you think of the cancer in your body, what do you imagine?" the doctor asked.

Dawn tipped her head and thought for a minute. "I see some strong, powerful force eating up my good blood," she confessed.

"Me, too!" Sandy chimed.

Dr. Kneeland smiled. "I thought so. But that's a wrong image, girls, a very wrong image. You see, the cancer is actually very weak and confused. It wanders and travels without unity and discipline. Now's the time for you to gather the forces of your own mind and start fighting it!" she stressed.

Both girls surveyed Dr. Kneeland skeptically. "Neither of you is a hopeless victim. Both of you can fight back," she said with enthusiasm.

"How?" they asked in unison.

"We call the technique 'Imaging,'" Dr. Kneeland explained. "Here's how it works. First, stop thinking about the negative. Concentrate on the positive. Gather your body's inner resources and picture them – literally – attacking the cancer cells and beating them up. Stomp on them! Punch them! Fight them! Picture the chemotherapy treatments helping you to do this.

"Sometimes, it helps to draw a picture of your personal image fighting the cancer cells. Hang that picture on the wall, concentrate on it every day, and *believe* that's what's happening inside you! A strong, positive attitude can help as much as all the medicines the doctors are giving you. I've done lots of research on this. It works and I can prove it."

"You mean, I'll get well if I want to badly enough?" Sandy asked.

"We believe that the 'will to live' has a scientific basis. You can fight your own disease and improve your life's quality during the course of the disease. And that enhances your chance of recovery," Dr. Kneeland told her.

Dawn turned the doctor's comments over and over in her mind. They made sense to her. Good health was the natural state of her body. Cancer was the unnatural state. The thought actually made her mad. *How dare those old cancer cells move into my body!* she thought.

"How do we do this 'Imaging'?" Dawn asked, eager to help in her own treatment.

The slender doctor smiled warmly. "I have a whole program for you. Certain steps toward relaxation are followed. Then you concentrate on turning your own bodily defenses against the invader. I will train you and help you every step of the way," she said.

Dr. Kneeland gave the girls sheets of papers outlining the Imaging process. Dawn scanned it quickly. It looked simple enough. "Just think positively," she said.

"Exactly!" Dr. Kneeland said.

"It seems too simple," Sandy drawled.

"Can I pray to get well, too?" Dawn asked.

"Absolutely! Don't let the cancer get strong. *You* get strong. *You* fight it. *You* imagine it as ugly and weak and frightened of medical treatment. Can you girls do that?" the doctor asked.

Dawn nodded, feeling renewed vitality and hope about getting well. "I wish I could draw," she mused. "I'd draw a picture of an army of teddy bears charging out to fight these green, gloppy looking blobs. My teddy bears would be riding white horses and carrying long lances like knights of the Round Table." She started giggling at the thought of Mr. Ruggers leading a brigade of pandas, potbellies, and fuzzy-wuzzies in her defense.

Dr. Kneeland snapped her fingers and applauded. "That's right, Dawn. You've got the idea. Fight! Don't let the cancer cells gain an inch. Fight them for every cell of your body!"

After the doctor left, Dawn and Sandy scanned the papers she'd left with them. Dawn was determined to follow the Imaging program faithfully. "At least I'll be doing *something* to help!" she told her pert roommate.

But the queasiness returned to her stomach that evening. Dawn crawled meekly into her bed and pulled the covers over her head, longing for the horrible nausea to pass.

Visiting hours brought some of her friends from school. Kim looked on the verge of tears and Rhonda looked scared. The silence between them stretched over several moments before Kim finally managed, "Gee . . . cancer . . . What a rotten deal!"

Don't feel sorry for me! Dawn thought. She didn't want their pity.

"Jake asked about you," Rhonda said, trying to fill up the awkwardness between them.

Dawn's heart gave a little flip-flop. "Jake Macka," Dawn said to herself. She had had a crush on him since the fifth grade. And now that she was sick, he asked about her. *Big deal*, she thought sourly.

"The . . . uh . . . cheerleaders made you this card," Rhonda said. She handed Dawn a home-made card filled with signatures of the twelve-member cheerleading squad.

"Thanks," she said and ran her hands across the surface.

"Mrs. Talbert says she'll come by to see you, too," Kim added.

"That'll be nice," Dawn said. But she secretly wished her Phys. Ed. teacher and cheerleading coach would not come to see her. She felt strange, lying in a hospital bed and trying to make small talk with friends who didn't understand her state of mind. She wished everyone would just stay away!

Finally, her friends left and Dawn lay back against the pillow and took deep breaths. Her mood had grown sullen and dark.

"Hard, isn't it?" asked Sandy from the next bed.

"What's hard?" Dawn asked.

"Seein' and bein' around normal people," Sandy answered. Dawn nodded, trying to rise above her depression.

"Half of them don't know what to say, and the other half say the wrong things," Sandy continued. "Bein' sick like this . . . nobody really knows what it's like. They say they understand, but they really don't." A small crack in Sandy's voice caused Dawn to blink hard against the sting in her own eyes.

"*We* understand," Dawn told Sandy fiercely.

"That Jake," Sandy ventured after a minute of silence. "Is he your boyfriend?"

"No," Dawn confessed. "I-I sort of like him, but he's not my boyfriend." Then she asked, "Do you have a boyfriend?"

Sandy's voice grew soft. "Sort of. A guy back home, Jason Jensen, kind of likes me . . ." Her voice trailed and Dawn noticed Sandy's cheeks blushing. She blushed slightly, too, remembering her own feelings about Jake.

"He . . . he kissed me once," Sandy added in a soft whisper. "It was real sweet, like he really meant it."

Dawn wished Jake had kissed her. Now that

she had cancer, he probably never would. The chemotherapy would make her ugly and sick. Probably no one would ever want to kiss her as long as she lived!

CHAPTER
4

The war against Dawn's cancer intensified. She took drugs by mouth and drugs by IVs. She half-suspected there were drugs in her food, whenever she could get food to stay down! The doctors and nurses were very kind. Her parents, friends, teachers and people from her church were also very kind and thoughtful. But it was Sandy, her good and constant friend and fellow victim, who made the difference in Dawn's state of mind.

Without Sandy, Dawn was sure she'd never survive. They shared their hurts, their fears and their hopes. Within a few weeks they became the best of friends, linked by the bond of their illness and their fierce determination to beat leukemia.

The first time Dawn met Sandy's parents, she felt overwhelmed. Mr. Chandler was a mountain of a man. He stood over six and a half feet tall. His legs reminded her of tree trunks. Mrs. Chandler was a tiny, petite woman who had a soft, pretty complexion and white-blonde hair like Sandy's.

"How's my darlin'?" Mr. Chandler's voice boomed from the doorway of their hospital room. Sandy squealed with delight and flung her arms open to him.

"Sandy's told me about you," he told Dawn, who openly stared at him. "My, my, you're hardly bigger than a June bug," he said, his accent causing her to smile shyly.

He eyed both of the girls critically. "They feedin' you girls proper? Neither of you look like you've had a decent meal in a month of Sundays."

"We're eatin' fine, Daddy," Sandy told him. "It's just that some of the drugs kind of make us sick."

His lips pressed together. Dawn got the feeling that under his cheerful words and broad smile, Mr. Chandler was very angry about Sandy being sick.

"That's right," Dawn added. "They have a special kitchen on this floor with a microwave and refrigerator and everything. Why, we can get pizza at midnight if we want it!"

"Pizza at midnight." Mr. Chandler made a face. "Doesn't sound too appetizin' to me."

"You do look a mite thin, sugar," Mrs. Chandler added. She patted her daughter's thin hand and smoothed Sandy's hair off her forehead.

"Now, Mama," Sandy said. "Don't you fret. They're takin' real good care of me."

But once the weekend was over and her parents had returned to West Virginia, Sandy confided, "My bein' sick is really hard on my Pa. He almost didn't send me to this hospital."

Dawn looked at her with surprise. "No kidding?" she asked.

"No kidding," she restated. "He was looking into those cancer clinics in Europe and Mexico. But Mama persuaded him to see Dr. Sinclair first." Sandy giggled. "My mama looks small and frail, but she's as stubborn as a mule when she sets her mind to somethin'."

Dawn giggled, too. "Well, I'm glad you're here. Who'd I have for a friend if you weren't?" she asked.

Sandy's face grew serious. "When we both leave here, let's write each other. Okay?"

Dawn agreed and felt relieved. Leaving the hospital *had* been on her mind, too. Sandy had become the best friend she'd ever known. And it was difficult to imagine not being around her every day. Dawn was glad they were going to keep in touch. She was glad they'd be able to write one another.

"Maybe we can even get together next summer for a visit," Dawn offered eagerly.

"That'd be real nice," Sandy drawled. "That is, if we're both around next summer," she added softly.

37

* * * * *

Dawn had allowed a few tears to spill the first time Rob came to visit. "Hi, Squirt," he said. And she slipped her arms around his waist and buried her face in his broad chest.

"How's college?" she asked, sniffing back her emotions at seeing him again.

"I'm knocking them dead," he said with a smile. "I have several girl friends," he added.

Dawn gasped. "But what about you and Debbie?" she asked. Dawn remembered how Debbie and Rob had dated all through high school. She secretly thought that her brother might marry Debbie someday.

"That was high school," Rob said. "College is different. There is so much going on that I can't be tied down to just one girl."

The idea amazed Dawn. She'd never even had a date and Rob was already dating lots of different girls. She wondered about herself. Would she still be able to date, have fun and go to college like Rob? She knew the leukemia hung over her future like a dark cloud.

That same day, Dr. Sinclair held a special meeting with her family. They listened as the big, blond doctor explained about the bone marrow transplant course of treatment.

"As you know," Dr. Sinclair began once Dawn's family had settled around her bed, "the bone marrow is where new blood cells are

38

formed. Sometimes, despite all the chemotherapy, we can't keep a patient in remission. At that point we consider a bone marrow transplant."

"I don't understand," Dawn told him.

"We take the marrow from a healthy donor and place it into your bones," he explained. "Hopefully, the new marrow begins functioning and making new blood cells."

"Why can't we do it now?" Dawn asked.

Dr. Sinclair smiled and shook his head. "It's not that simple. It's a whole different type of treatment that we only do when conventional treatment doesn't work. Also," he said, "we have to have a donor from the patient's family, preferably a sibling. So, while you're all here, we'd like to do some blood tests. How about it?" He looked from Mr. and Mrs. Rochelle to Rob. All agreed enthusiastically.

"You'd give me your bone marrow?" Dawn asked Rob shyly once they were alone.

"Absolutely!" Rob said, chucking her on her chin. "I gave you the chicken pox, didn't I? I can spare bone marrow for you, too."

"Thanks," was all she could whisper. She felt deep gratitude for the love he was showing her. Rob . . . so big and strong . . . and healthy.

* * * * *

The days in the hospital stretched into weeks.

Time became fluid, flowing around tests, treatments, meals, T.V. and time in the activity room. Dawn quickly discovered that the Oncology floor was full of kids.

There were little kids who shrieked and cried, big kids who tried to hide from the nurses, and kids like her and Sandy. There was one girl of 16, who left after Dawn had been there two weeks, and a boy of 15, who had also gone home after a few weeks of treatment.

"It's different for everyone," Nurse Fredia explained while she made up Dawn's bed one morning. "Some kids come in here, go into remission after the first round of drugs, go home and never return. Some come in, go through many rounds of treatment and relapse in six months. There's no predicting how the disease will effect any one person."

Dawn practiced her Imaging therapy regularly, focusing on mental pictures of her teddy bear army destroying entire armies of ugly green globs. She pictured Mr. Ruggers leading bear brigades through her veins and arteries and blasting every green glob that got in his path. The technique was most helpful when the chemotherapy made her very sick. "The drugs are my friends!" she told herself over and over.

She and Sandy went to the activity room every day. It was well equipped with games, toys, projects and even video game machines. These helped break up the monotony of the long days. The play therapist, Joan Clarke, was always coming up with things to keep the patients busy.

One time she organized a Popcorn Party. The kids on the Oncology floor popped gallons of corn and then used what they didn't eat in art projects. Dawn drew a teddy bear on poster board and glued hundreds of kernels of fluffy popcorn to him.

"He looks like he has a bad case of acne," Sandy mused.

"I thought it looked more like dandruff," Dawn giggled, holding the stiff board at arm's length.

"Now this is a work of art," Sandy said, displaying her own creation. She'd strung individual kernels of popcorn onto a string and sprinkled the entire necklace with sparkling glitter. Every time she turned the string of popcorn around, it caught the reflection from the overhead lights and shimmered.

"Not bad," Dawn admitted grudgingly. Then she burst out laughing. "When Jason takes you to a movie, wear that and he won't have to spend his money on popcorn. Think of what a cheap date you'd be!"

Sandy joined in, laughing, then said, "Here, Jason, won't you have a nibble off my neck?"

They collasped into helpless peals of laughter, until everyone else in the activity room started giggling along with them. Soon, someone tossed a kernel across the room, bouncing it off someone else's head. The "victim" retaliated. In a matter of minutes, the entire room erupted into a melee of flying popcorn.

Kids screeched and roared. Their laughter resounded in the halls as fistfuls of light, fluffy popcorn sailed through the room. Dawn quickly fashioned a popcorn bomb by clumping a ball together in her hands with glue. Then she flung it wildly at an opponent. The gooey mess came apart in the air and landed with a sticky splat on a boy's bald head.

He wiped it off and swore revenge. Dawn squealed and dived under a table. He scrambled under it, too, armed with a handful of popcorn that he managed to stuff down the back of her robe. "I give up!" she cried, helpless with laughter. "I give up!"

A blast from a whistle caused the commotion to stop in mid-stream. Nurse Fredia and four other nurses stood in the doorway, their eyes wide with amazement.

"What happened?" Nurse Fredia gasped, holding a whistle in her hand. Guiltily, everybody looked at each other.

The nurse tried to look harsh, but everyone could see the laugh lines starting at the corners of her mouth. The other nurses buried their mouths in the palms of their hands to keep from breaking out into open laughter.

"You're not mad?" Jimmy Porter, a ten-year-old, asked.

"Tell you what," Nurse Fredia said to the room of hard-breathing kids. "I'm going to shut this door for twenty minutes. When I return, I expect the Good Fairies to have arrived and completely put this room back in order. Is it a deal?"

Everybody nodded and murmured, "Yes, ma'am."

She left. The cleanup was accomplished in ten minutes. Dawn remembered the day for a long time to come. She remembered it not only because of the fun she'd had at the popcorn party, but because that very night a long clump of her beautiful auburn hair fell out in her hand.

CHAPTER
5

The next morning, another hunk of her hair lay against the clean white pillowcase. "Oh, no!" Dawn wailed. "It's starting! I'm really going bald!"

Sandy patted Dawn's arm and confided. "Mine's fallin' out too. I-I didn't want to say anythin', but look." The pretty blonde-haired girl dipped her head and Dawn saw a sparse area at her crown.

Dawn fought down her panic and despair and swallowed hard. "I guess it's going to happen to both of us," she said.

"Guess so," Sandy confirmed.

It was bad for Dawn. But it wasn't nearly so bad now that Sandy was going through it with her. "Misery loves company," her grandmother had always said. Dawn understood what she meant.

"I guess I won't be needin' these anymore," Sandy said, opening the drawer next to her bed and pulling out a small cardboard box.

45

Dawn lifted the lid and saw Sandy's entire collection of hair combs, barrettes and hair ribbons. Sandy owned combs in almost every color imaginable — blue, green, red, purple, yellow — beautiful colors that coordinated with all her clothes. Now the combs would be useless. Dawn felt bitterness welling up in her. How cruel it was to go bald at 13! How awful it was to be sick all the time from the effects of the chemotherapy! How terrible it was to be tired and depressed, have sores in your mouth, bruises all over your body and to be so thin you could count your own ribs!

"It isn't fair!" she said aloud. "It just isn't fair!"

"It's just hair," Sandy said with a shrug and stuffed the box back into the drawer. "Everyone says it'll grow back."

"I'm calling Mom," Dawn said. "Maybe she can think of something."

Meggie Rochelle *did* think of something. She arrived that very afternoon with Mrs. Cooper. The heavy-set woman with the pleasant face and ready smile was a member of Dawn's church and owned her own beauty salon. She arrived with two small duffle bags. One was filled with hair grooming equipment. The other was stuffed with wigs.

"Now, let's see what Dorothy Cooper can do about this 'problem' you're having," the woman said.

She went to work on Dawn first. Mrs. Cooper dragged a comb lightly through Dawn's once-thick auburn hair. Large clumps landed on the floor with a gentle plip-plop sound. Dawn winced. But Mrs. Cooper worked quickly. She snipped, cut and shaped the remaining hair into a very short bob.

"This will help some," she told Dawn. "At least it will be less noticeable for a while."

Dawn surveyed herself in the mirror. "I look like Mr. T," she lamented.

Sandy giggled. "My turn!" she cried, eagerly taking Dawn's place in the chair.

Mrs. Cooper went to work immediately on Sandy. Within 20 minutes she had pruned Sandy's long, silky white-blonde hair into soft layers. "Yours isn't as thick as Dawn's," Mrs. Cooper said. "So it'll look thinner a lot sooner."

Sandy tipped her head at her mirror reflection and nodded her approval. "I kind of like it," she mused. "I've always had such pitifully thin hair. It takes forever to grow. It's kind of cute real short."

Dawn's mom and Mrs. Cooper agreed. "Well, whenever you get tired of your own hair," the hair dresser began, "then try one of these." She lifted the second duffle bag onto Dawn's bed and unzipped it. She pulled out wigs in all styles, colors and lengths.

Sandy squealed with delight. "Oh, Dawn! Look at this! I've always wanted to be a redhead!" Sandy scooped up a bright red wig, bushy with tight curls, and pulled it onto her head.

Dawn laughed. "You look like a clown!" Dawn cried. Then she jerked on a jet-black wig in a smooth mid-length that barely covered her ears.

"You look like an elf!" Sandy teased. "How about this?" Sandy cried, pulling on a chestnut-colored hair piece that cascaded to her shoulders.

" 'Rapunzel, Rapunzel, let down your hair!' " Dawn quoted laughingly.

"Would you like to try something that looks bizarre?" Mrs. Cooper asked, her blue eyes twinkling. She held up a pink and blue hairpiece that poked up in thick spikes.

"You could put out somebody's eye," Mrs. Rochelle gasped.

"Don't you think it's me?" Sandy squealed and pulled it onto her head. The effect was so comical that everyone burst into laughter.

The two girls rummaged through the pile of wigs. They eventually settled on two casual, undramatic styles that looked cute and natural on each of them. Sandy chose one more golden than her naturally blonde hair color. And Dawn chose one in a dark brown, curly style. They snuggled the wigs securely on their heads and primped in front of the mirror.

The afternoon had been fun, but tiring. Dawn felt her energy reserves ebbing as her mom prepared to leave with Mrs. Cooper. "Thanks, Mom," she said.

"Yeah, thanks a whole bunch," Sandy added. "It makes going bald a whole lot easier."

Mrs. Rochelle squeezed both girls tightly, blinking back some unbidden tears. "You two are wonderful kids," she said. "I'll do anything to make this easier for you. Anything!" she added for emphasis.

Dawn watched her mom and Mrs. Cooper hurry away. Then she and Sandy left their room to show off their brand new hair at the nurses station. Afterward, Dawn fell into an exhausted sleep ... a sleep so deep and dreamless that she didn't even wake for supper.

* * * * *

The chemotherapy continued to take its toll on Dawn. In six weeks she'd lost 15 pounds. Her clothes hung limply on her five-foot frame. Her bones and joints ached. The nurses had to put a thick lambskin pad under her pelvis so that her hip bones wouldn't jab and bruise her skin from the inside whenever she slept at night.

A fine rash covered her arms and legs, a reaction to the combinations of drugs. Her blood vessels erupted, causing deep purple bruises to appear like splotches on her body. Her skin took on a blackish cast as the drugs affected the pigmentation. Scabs formed on her lips and she could no longer bear to look at her own reflection in the mirror.

"It isn't me, Mom," Dawn told her mother whenever she saw her mirror image. "It isn't me."

Mrs. Rochelle held Dawn's hand tightly and smoothed her daughter's dry, papery skin with her palm. "I know, baby," she whispered. "And once you go into remission, you'll get your regular face and body back. I promise."

Remission. To Dawn, the word sounded like an unobtainable goal, a utopia that she would never reach. Remission, she had been told, was like an island of peace and comfort, away from the drugs and chemicals that burned and hurt going into her veins. These were the drugs that caused her to retch and heave until she felt like collapsing. These drugs caused her to feel so weak and tired that she could hardly lift her head from her pillow.

She tried to eat, but the drugs caused foods to taste peculiar, odd, strange. Sweet things turned bitter in her mouth. Chocolate tasted so horrible that the thought of brownies and fudge made her gag. Yet sometimes she developed cravings both bizarre and weird.

The nurses were always ready to accommodate any craving, any request for food at anytime of the day or night. Dawn ate tacos at 3 A.M. and spaghetti for breakfast. She managed a watermelon-flavored milkshake one afternoon and thought it tasted wonderful.

Her parents stood by her. They were always there, always comforting, always loving. They answered her questions, told her the truth about her illness and kept her informed about school, church and world events. Usually, she was too sick to care. But it helped knowing that they tried so hard to keep up her spirits.

Sandy suffered the same agonies. When it was especially bad for one or the other, the one least affected would help the other. They read poetry to one another. They told each other long, silly stories about school and childhood fantasies.

"When I get married," Sandy would say, "I want two children, a boy and a girl. I'll call the boy Christopher and the girl, Dawn . . . ."

"I'm going to college just like Rob," Dawn would tell her friend. "I'm going to be a lawyer. Daddy always said I could argue the fuzz off a peach . . . ."

"Do you think Jason will ever want to kiss me again?" Sandy would ask.

"Do you think I'll ever be able to be on the cheerleading squad again?" Dawn would counter.

On the days when they both felt decent, they struggled to keep up with their respective school work. Dawn was determined to pass to the eighth grade. Her cancer was not going to hold her back an entire school year! She took the tests her teachers prepared for her and her mother brought to the hospital. She even managed to complete an English term paper. But algebra had to wait until she felt better. She simply couldn't manage to grasp it in her weakened state.

Rob wrote. He called often. Rhonda called, too. But her friends eventually stopped coming to the hospital. They told one another that the sight of Dawn was just too depressing. Secretly, Dawn was relieved that they stopped visiting. It was disheartening to be around them. They didn't understand. No one but Sandy *really* understood what she was going through.

So, Dawn waited, accepting her therapy and taking her medications. She waited for that wonderful day when the bone marrow aspirations, the blood tests, the red count, the white count and the platelet count would all show that she was finally in remission. It would be then that her body and her mind were winning the war against leukemia. She would be winning the battle for control of her life.

"You have a fever," Nurse Fredia said. She slipped the end of the electronic thermometer out of Dawn's mouth and flicked the white sheath off into the garbage can.

"So what's new?" Dawn asked weakly. The chemotherapy had caused her to have fevers before.

Nurse Fredia's cool hands brushed Dawn's brow and her eyes looked worried and concerned. "I think this one's different," she told

Dawn. "You may be coming down with an infection."

Dawn's heart gave a little lurch. She knew it was dangerous to get an infection while taking chemotherapy. The powerful drugs killed cancer cells, but they also killed and weakened normal cells. She simply didn't have the inner resources to fight off an infection, not even a simple cold.

"What does that mean?" Dawn asked through dry, cracked lips feeling suddenly weak, then hot, then cold.

"I'm calling Dr. Sinclair," Nurse Fredia told her and left the room.

In minutes, doctors seemed to materialize around her bed. Hands probed, voices whispered, sounds rose and receded all around her.

"Dawn!" Dr. Sinclair was calling her name. She struggled to speak, but no sound came out. Why couldn't she answer him? She wanted to.

"Dawn," his voice said from far away. "We're going to move you, Dawn. We're taking you down to Intensive Care so that we can monitor you more closely."

She wanted to tell him, "No." She wanted to let him know that she was fine right here in her own room. But she was too weak to respond, too weak and tired and cold and hot.

From far away she heard Sandy say her name. And it sounded like she was crying . . . .

CHAPTER
6

Someone lifted her onto another bed, someone with strong, cool hands. The bed started to roll. Dawn was conscious of moving out of her room, onto an elevator and down a long hallway. Overhead, the lights flowed past like a stream. She shut her eyes against the glare and the intensity of their brightness.

Her head hurt. It pounded, throbbed and ached. It felt like it weighed a ton and she couldn't manage to move it from side to side. The rolling bed stopped in another room. This room was quiet. The lights were very dim.

The hands lifted her again onto another bed. There were machines and a curtain all around the bed. She felt surrounded by nurses she didn't recognize. Where was Nurse Fredia? Dawn felt confused and disoriented.

Someone attached little metal cups to her chest. Wires led from the cups to a machine next to her bed. The compact machine sounded blip-

blip-blip as a tiny green line journeyed across its television-shaped face over and over.

"That's the signal of your heartbeat," a voice explained.

What a funny place to keep my heartbeat, Dawn thought. Why would they want to see her heartbeat? Didn't they know she had leukemia?

Someone else stuck something in her arm. Dawn moaned and felt something warm flood through her. An upside-down bottle clanked next to her bed on a metal stand. Dawn saw it and wondered why it was filled with red liquid. Her chemotherapy wasn't red . . . .

"We're giving you blood," the nurse told her. "Your blood count is very low. We're giving you antibiotics, too."

Dawn half-heard her. *Have they told my mom and dad?* she wondered. *What will they think when they come to visit me tomorrow and find my bed empty? They'll be worried. Sandy will tell them,* she assured herself. *Sandy's a good friend . . .*

A slow comfortable lethargy began to spread through her limbs. She felt like she was floating, drifting down a river toward peaceful sleep. There was no pain, no noise, only the sweet, wonderful sensation of floating up, up and up into a quiet, cool realm of dark bliss.

* * * * *

Dawn Rochelle had little memory of the time she spent in Intensive Care. It was mostly impressions and dream fantasies. She was sometimes aware of everything; sometimes aware of nothing. There were many nurses and doctors. It seemed as if someone was always in the room with her.

She couldn't talk. They had shoved a tube down her throat and it prohibited her from speaking. The monitor next to her bed kept sending the green line signaling that her heart beat regularly. The tubes, bottles, bags and syringes all testified to the gravity of her illness.

She remembered her parents floating in and out of the room. She remembered nurses, technicians and doctors. She recalled her minister standing next to her bed and it occurred to her that maybe God would hear his prayers for her. She didn't care what happened to her. She was too sick to care.

Rob came. "Hi, Squirt." His voice came from the end of a long tunnel. In her mind, she was walking toward him through a field of flowers. A teddy bear on a large white horse stopped next to her and offered her a ride.

"Mr. Ruggers!" she gasped in her dream state. "What are you doing here?"

He said nothing. Teddy bears can't talk. She should have remembered that. But he pulled her up onto the horse behind him. She tightened her

57

arms around his plump, fuzzy waist and rode with him through the tall grass on his great white steed.

They came to a stream which they crossed. They came to an old castle. It was covered with moss and vines, and the stones looked ancient and crumbling. "Look!" Dawn cried, pointing up to a turret of the old castle.

A girl leaned out, a pretty girl with long, long white-blonde hair. "I know her," Dawn told Mr. Ruggers. "You need to get her down," she told the bear.

The great white horse reared and the pretty girl called, "I'm Rapunzel. Can you get me down? The wicked witch leukemia has locked me up here. I want to go home."

Mr. Ruggers raised his lance. Dawn pressed herself closer to his warm bear body, except he was no longer a bear. Suddenly, he'd turned into Jake Macka from her school. She blushed and let go. She felt awkward hugging Jake so tightly.

"Dawn! Dawn!" Her mother's voice was calling her away from the castle. She drifted back from the castle wall and off the white horse and floated like an autumn leaf down onto a bed in a hospital room.

She struggled to speak, but the tube down her throat wouldn't let her. "It's all right, Honey," her mother said. "Don't talk. I love you, Dawn. Daddy loves you. Sandy says to hurry up and get well. She misses you."

Dawn nodded ever so slowly, and then drifted back to sleep.

One day, she awoke, the last of her stupor and half-consciousness gone. Everything hurt, but she was alert and aware and sore. And she was hungry.

They removed the tube from her throat. "Welcome back," Dr. Sinclair told her. "You've been a mighty sick little girl. But you're going to be fine now. We've licked the infection and you're recovering."

Dawn tried to say, "Thanks." But her throat was too sore.

"The tube," Dr. Sinclair explained.

Her parents arrived and the expression on their faces told her that Dr. Sinclair had been truthful with her. She was going to be fine. Her mom's eyes filled with bright tears as she kissed her daughter's forehead. Her dad held her hand and said, "I knew you'd pull through, baby. You're a fighter."

Dawn wanted to get out of Intensive Care. She wanted to return to her room on the Oncology floor. She wanted to see Sandy again. She wanted to be free of the ICU ward, its monitors, "blips," tubes and IV bottles. Two days later, she got her wish. They returned her to her regular hospital room. Nurse Fredia personally came for her, pushing Dawn in a wheelchair onto the Oncology floor.

Someone had strung a long banner across the

hallway. It read: "Welcome Back, Dawn!" Many of the kids stood by the doorways of their rooms and waved to her as she glided down the hall. Nurse Fredia delivered her to her room and said, "We missed you, Dawn! Welcome back!"

Her room was filled with flowers in baskets and vases, and dish gardens of green plants. Dawn blinked and gasped with surprise. She hadn't expected such a reception. Sandy greeted her with squeals of joy. They hugged each other warmly. "I've missed you so much!" her friend cried. "Oh, I'm so glad you're back!"

Dawn smiled, still feeling weak. "You have a pile of cards and letters in the drawer of your bedside table," Nurse Fredia told her. "I think half of the state of Ohio has written you."

"I'll look at them later," Dawn said, feeling overwhelmed by the outpouring of affection people had shown her. Nurse Fredia settled her in bed. Once everybody left, Dawn asked Sandy to tell her what had happened during her two-week stay in Intensive Care.

Sandy burbled on and on. Dawn lay listening, letting Sandy's words wash over her, happy to be near her friend again. After a while, Sandy grew silent. When she spoke again, it was in quiet, almost shy tones. "I-I made you somethin'," she said.

"In the activity room?" Dawn asked.

"Yes," Sandy confirmed. And she handed Dawn a rolled-up piece of poster board.

Gingerly, Dawn unrolled the stiff paper board. On it Sandy had drawn a teddy bear army attacking clumps and clusters of bright green globs. Dawn gasped with surprise. "My Imaging picture!" she said. "Oh, Sandy! It's super, just like I imagined it! Thanks so much!"

"I-I thought it might help you. And ... and it's somethin' for you to remember me by when we both go home," she added.

"I'm going to hang it right here on that wall across from my bed. And when I go home, I'm going to hang it up in my room. It's really special, Sandy, mostly because you drew it," Dawn said.

Sandy smiled and gave a modest shrug. "When you were gone ... in Intensive Care ... I thought about what a good friend you've become to me. I-I always want you to remember me ... " her voice trailed.

"I'll never forget you," Dawn said fiercely. "Never! You're the best friend ever. And we're going to celebrate with a reunion every year after we go into remission. So start planning on it!"

Sandy smiled a bit sadly. "I hope we can, Dawn. I hope we can be friends forever!" she said.

"Forever!" Dawn said. "And once we've been in remission for five years, we'll celebrate by taking a long vacation together," Dawn assured her. "Because after five years, even Dr. Sinclair says we're cured."

Sandy nodded and drawled, "Here's to our five-year vacation trip!" Sandy Chandler and Dawn Rochelle toasted each other and their futures with styrofoam cups filled with warm pop while the hospital routine settled in around them.

CHAPTER
7

The next morning Dawn looked at herself in the bathroom mirror. It was a mistake. For a full minute, she did not recognize the person who stared back at her. In fact, if the image had not lifted its hand to touch its face whenever she did, she would not have believed that it was truly herself.

Dawn thought she looked like a victim of a concentration camp, gaunt and thin. Her skin was stretched across her bones. Its color, pale and ashen, seemed transparent. It looked as if it might tear if she pressed it too hard. Her lips were chapped and cracked and what was left of her hair was dull and flat.

"I am ugly," she told her mother, "really ugly."

"You're alive," her mother reminded her. "Looks will come back. Remember, 'Beauty is in the eye of the beholder,' " she quoted. "I think you're absolutely gorgeous." Dawn knew her mother was right. Once the chemotherapy was complete, her looks would return.

Dawn went through the stacks and stacks of letters and cards. Most were from people in her church, distant relatives and friends of her parents. Many were from kids at school. Her entire English class had written. "It was probably a writing assignment," Dawn told Sandy. "You know, like the kind teachers always give you at the start of school: 'What I Did on My Summer Vacation.' "

Sandy giggled. "I know. Boy, am I gonna have a lot to write about next year!" she laughed.

But one card, one very special card was from Jake Macka. Dawn's heart thumped as she read it and her hands trembled slightly. It was a cute card with a picture of a bear on it. *How'd Jake know about my liking bears?* she wondered. Inside, under the printed words, Jake had written:

Dawn,

Get well soon. Maybe I'll see you at the skating rink sometime this summer.

Jake

She clutched the card to her chest and savored his words and his memory . . . "the skating rink." Once she got home, she'd make a special trip to go there . . . once her hair grew back, and her body curves came back. Jake . . . tall, slim, with black hair and brown eyes . . . . She remembered how thick and long his eyelashes were. It was fun to think that he *really* wanted to see her. She hoped his card wasn't just an assignment and that he really meant it.

Dawn's illness had set her cancer therapy back by weeks. Therefore, a new schedule of drugs for Dawn began immediately. They were potent drugs and wonder drugs designed to stop the relentless spread of her leukemia. Dawn's days melted into one another. They dissolved and disappeared into one long continuous ebb and flow of time. Tests and more tests punctuated the hours. Drugs and more drugs splintered the day from the night. It was the same for Sandy.

Then one day, the lab reports came back for Sandy that said: "Remission." The elusive dream had been attained for her. The leukemia had been checked. Remission had been achieved. Maintenance drug programs had been arranged. And Sandy Chandler was going home.

"You write me, you hear?" Sandy demanded her last day in the hospital.

Dawn struggled to hold back her tears and nodded numbly to her friend. "I will," she promised. "And you write me. Tell me what to expect when I get back home."

Mr. Chandler gathered up his daughter's belongings. Three months of books, magazines, plants and stuffed animals were piled into cardboard boxes. Dawn tried not to notice from the corner of her eye. It was too painful. Sandy was leaving. She was staying.

"It'll happen for you, too," her friend told her. Sandy's mother had bought her new jeans and a top for her homecoming. Sandy was still very thin, but her color was again bright in her fair cheeks and her wig made her look older than her 13 years.

"I know," Dawn said, fighting to keep her voice from cracking. "I'll look at the picture you made for me every day, and I'll think of you," Dawn assured her.

"We're ready, Hon!" her father's voice boomed. He looked coiled, like an animal ready to spring from a cage. "Now you take good care of yourself, Dawn," he directed. "Maybe you could come and visit us next summer."

"I'd like that," Dawn said.

Then she watched as Sandy followed her parents out of the door toward her freedom. The late morning sun cut through the window and filled the room with bright, warm light. But inside, Dawn felt cold and empty. For the first time in two and a half months, she was alone.

She fought to keep her tears of depression from spilling down her cheeks. She clutched the bedsheets tightly in her fists. Her mom would come soon, she knew. Maybe she could make the hurt and loneliness go away. "I won't cry!" she told herself fiercely. "I should be happy. Sandy is in remission. I should be grateful and not be laying around feeling sorry for myself."

Wiping the back of her hand across her eyes, Dawn leaned forward and buzzed the nurses' station. In minutes, Nurse Fredia appeared. "What's up?" she asked.

"I'd like a milk shake, please," Dawn said.

Nurse Fredia broke into a broad smile. "Good! Excellent! What flavor?"

"Strawberry," Dawn said. "Make it double thick and put some of that protein powder in it, too. The sooner I get out of this place, the better," she added with determination.

* * * * *

Within four days, a letter arrived from Sandy. Eagerly, Dawn tore it open and read the neat, flowing writing.

Dear Dawn,

It's strange being back home again. Nothing has changed. Everything has changed. For a while everything was so exciting . . . seeing old friends, making my own sandwiches, you know.

My folks treat me like I was made of glass. They stick to me like white on rice. Sometimes I just have to go into my room and shut the door for privacy. The only one who treats me normally is my little brother, Paul. He still fights and argues with me.

It's kind of scary, too, being so far from the hospital and all the nurses and doctors. Sometimes I worry about what I'll do if I have a relapse. Or I wonder what will happen if I get real sick like you did from some other germs.

Some of my friends came over to welcome me home. After about fifteen minutes, we didn't have anything left to talk about. It seemed so strange being around them. We don't have anything in common anymore. Maybe things will change when school starts. I hope so.

Mom took me shopping, too. I've lost so much weight that nothing fits my skinny body. We went up to the big shopping mall and guess who I saw? Yep! Jason. We kind of stood looking at each other for a few minutes. He didn't know what to say and neither did I. Of course, all his big, dumb friends were standing around too, razzing him and making it even worse.

He looked like all he wanted to do was run away. I wonder if he remembers that time he kissed me? Honest, Dawn, I do

wonder if things will ever be the same
again. Ever!

Write soon!

Love,
Sandy

Dawn read and reread Sandy's letter. She
understood her friend's feelings of loneliness
and isolation. Was it going to be the same for her?
Would her friends accept her once again? Would
she still get to do all the things she did before?

Dawn kept herself as busy as possible in the
hospital. She wrote letters to Sandy, Rob, and
her grandparents. She learned how to knit and
made a pull-on ski cap for one of the little girls on
the floor. She grew more ambitious and started
knitting an afghan as a Christmas gift for her
mom. She figured it would take her until
Christmas to complete it.

She worked in the activity room with the
smaller kids, playing games and helping with arts
and crafts. "We're certainly going to miss you
around here," Joan, the play therapist, told
her.

"I'll miss the people," Dawn confessed. "But I
hate this place. I'll never miss it."

"You know," Joan said as Dawn cut out paper
shapes one afternoon. "You should plan to come
to Cancer camp this summer."

"Cancer camp?" Dawn asked, lowering the

scissors and surveying the pert therapist.

"We reach out to kids with cancer, all types of cancer," Joan said. "It's held every August at a beautiful camp facility in the country. There's no roughing it either. There are air-conditioned cabins, a swimming pool, horse stables . . . only the best.

"It's a lot of fun with an opportunity to meet many kids like yourself. Your age group, twelve to eighteen year olds, spends two weeks there. And they really have a good time! They just play, play, play." She beamed Dawn a big smile. "Why don't I give you some literature? Then talk it over with your parents and think about coming. I know you'll have a terrific time!" Joan added.

Dawn nodded, but inside she knew that Cancer camp was the last place in the world she wanted to go! Once she got well, she was going back to the world of normal people. She was never going to be around sick people again. Never!

"That would be nice," she told Joan, then promptly dismissed the idea completely.

One week later, her tests results came back with positive results. "Remission," Dr. Sinclair told Dawn and her parents. "I think it's safe to plan to send you home and make room for some sick kids." He smiled and Dawn's heart did a flip-flop. It had happened for her, too. Like Sandy, she'd attained remission. Her imaginary teddy bear army, the chemotherapy, the doctors and nurses had all achieved their goal. They'd beaten down the leukemia and stopped its spread in her body.

"I'm going home," she told Nurse Fredia later that day. "I'm really going home!" To herself, she added, "Ready or not, World, here I come!"

CHAPTER
8

As Dawn drove home with her parents, she understood how Rip Van Winkle must have felt when he'd awakened from his years of long sleep. When Dawn had gone into the hospital, it had been April. The air was crisp, fresh and mild. The trees were newly decorated with the bright green color of late spring. The flower beds were alive with crocuses, geraniums and lilies.

Now, it was mid-July. The air was hot and heavy with the humidity of summer. The trees' leaves were full, dark green and mature. Summer roses and Queen Anne's Lace adorned hedges and yards. Dawn Rochelle had lost three months of her life. It was as if she'd gone into hibernation and come out into another time, a slightly different world.

The quiet neighborhood surrounded her home, the paint slightly peeling. Her dad halted the car in the driveway. The grass needed cutting and the front porch seemed smaller than she remembered it. Inside, her eyes swept over the familiar things from her childhood . . . her mother's matched Tiffany lamps . . . the portrait of her great-grandmother on the dining room wall.

She climbed the stairs to her bedroom, slowly, catching her breath every few steps. Her muscles were weak from disuse. She'd have to work on regaining strength in her flaccid muscles. She ran her hand along the smooth, dark wood banister. Her eyes took in the colors of her home, so different from the hospital's green and soft yellow to which she had grown accustomed.

Her bedroom was just as she'd left it, except for the giant bouquet of flowers perched on her dressing table. The card read: Welcome home! Mom and Dad.

"Thanks," she whispered. "They're beautiful."

Tears glistened in her mom's eyes and her dad cleared his throat. "You hungry?" he asked.

"No," she said. "I-I'd just like to be alone for a while."

"Of course," they said and left her to settle into her old patterns.

The unpacking went slowly as she stopped to rest every few minutes. Dawn decided she'd begin a regular exercise program before school started. She wanted to be strong enough to resume all her school activities once the new term started.

She put away her memorabilia from the hospital. She hung the poster Sandy had drawn directly across from her bed, so that she could see it first thing in the morning and the last thing at night. She caressed her numerous teddy bears and took Mr. Ruggers from his perch on the shelf and hugged him tightly to her.

"Did you miss me?" she asked the time-worn bear. She thought of Sandy, of Nurse Fredia, and of Dr. Sinclair. They seemed so far away.

Neighbors came to visit, to welcome her home. Her grandparents called. Rob sent her a box of candy by special messenger. He was staying in East Lansing for the summer, working and attending a few summer classes. She missed him.

It took a few days, but Dawn settled into her former life as if no time had passed, as if nothing was different, except that now she took medicine every day. Now she rested every afternoon. And now she ate several small meals a day instead of three large ones.

Her girl friends came by ... Kim, Rhonda, and Jill. "Kathy's parents dragged her off on vacation," Rhonda said. "She was desperate to stay here, too. Just when school got out Nate Hutchinson began to notice her. And then she has to go off for the summer!"

A chorus of sympathetic sighs went up. Dawn tried to get into the flow of the conversation, but she felt out of step, out of sync with her old crowd. *Hey ... I almost died!* she thought. It was hard to get excited about Kathy missing a summer romance with Nate. Sandy's words returned to Dawn. "We don't have anything in common any more . . . ."

It was hard to get back into the swing of her old life. So much had changed. She felt older, more seasoned. Things that were once very important, were no longer important. She felt at loose ends.

Another letter from Sandy arrived:

Dear Dawn,

I was glad to get your letter telling me you'd gone home. It takes a few days to readjust, but once things get back to normal, it seems like you never left in the first place.

Time keeps dragging by for me. My folks still won't let do too much. They act as if I'll break or something! We're driving over to Washington, D.C. for a family vacation. I've never been to the Capital before so I'm looking forward to it. (Actually I'm looking forward to ANYTHING that gets me out of this house!)

I'll write you some postcards. You keep writing me here at my house. Miss you.

Love,

Sandy

Dawn exercised regularly. Her summer days were broken by visits to the hospital as an outpatient. They tested her blood, her bone marrow and evaluated her medicines and test results. Gratefully, her remission remained in force. She visited the Oncology floor once. But it was depressing, so she decided not to visit again. She was getting well. The kids there were sick. She didn't like being reminded of her weeks of therapy.

"Want to go to the Mall tomorrow?" Rhonda called to ask one night. "We thought we'd do some shopping, eat lunch and go to a movie. It'll be like old times," she added.

"Sure," Dawn said. "Old times" . . . *but not exactly.*

The girls arrived at 10 A.M. as the stores were opening. The air-conditioned comfort of the Mall felt good. Already, the August heat had begun to wilt the air.

They browsed from store to store, trying on jeans, mini-dresses and ribbed sweaters for the fall. New colors, in confectionary shades, beckoned to Dawn. She chose a pullover in frosted blue and an oxford shirt in frothy green. Her wig covered her own thickening cap of regrown hair. By September, she knew she could go without it and the new colors would look super with her natural hair color.

They ordered hamburgers and chocolate shakes at a small cafe-style restaurant. The chocolate tasted good to Dawn again. They bought yogurt cones at an ice cream parlor. Dawn followed Kim, Rhonda, and Jill obediently. She listened to their giggles and gossip. She was part of them, yet separate. She was like them, yet different. It was an odd sensation.

The movie at the Mall was crowded. Kids milled around the lobby waiting for the early show to let out. Dawn bought popcorn and waited for her change. A boy next to her asked, "Dawn? Is that you, Dawn?"

She turned, surprised, and looked up into the dark brown eyes of Jake Macka. Her heart thudded.

"Hi, Jake," she said. The noise and the people around her receded into the buttery-smelling air.

He shuffled. "I—uh—I heard you were home." His Adam's apple bobbed as he swallowed. "You okay?" he asked.

She nodded, conscious of his nearness, feeling both shy and excited. "I sure liked the card you sent me. It was nice of you," Dawn said, smiling.

He dropped his eyes and scanned the bystanders quickly. *I shouldn't have reminded him,* she thought. *I've embarrassed him.*

He shrugged. "Are you coming back to school this fall?"

"Sure." Her palms were sweating and her wig felt hot and smothering. The cashier returned with Dawn's change. She took it, grateful for something to do with her hands. "How'd your baseball team do?" she asked. He was a star on a city league team. She recalled how handsome he looked in his uniform.

"We won the league, but lost in the county finals," he said.

"Too bad," she said, then added quickly, "I mean, I'm glad you won, but sorry you lost." *Dumb!* she thought.

"Well . . . " Jake said. "I guess I'd better go."

She stepped back to allow him to pass and landed on a little boy's toe. He jumped. She jumped. Jake laughed and she joined him, self-consciously.

"I'll see you around," he told her, then disappeared into a throng of people.

"Yeah, see you," she echoed.

"Were you talking to Jake?" Jill asked, coming up next to her.

Dawn nodded. "He just wanted to say hello," she said. "It was nothing." But Jill eyed her skeptically. Dawn took a handful of popcorn and ignored her friend's curious stare.

"He's cute," Jill said. Dawn nodded and followed her to join the other girls. They walked, single file into the darkened theater. Dawn wished she were sitting with Jake. She wished he'd hold her hand. She wished . . . she wished . . .

* * * * *

Two things arrived for Dawn in the mail in the middle of August. One was a letter from Sandy. The second was a brochure on Cancer camp and a brief note from Joan Clarke.

Here's that brochure I promised you in the hospital! Talk it over with your parents and plan to attend. You'll have a good time. I promise!

Joan.

P.S. I'll be your counselor.

The letter from Sandy described her trip to Washington. It read in part . . .

The Smithsonian was awesome! All those diamonds, emeralds and rubies! You can't imagine how much they're worth. The dinosaur room was super, too. It contained bones of animals as big as a room!

But now that I'm home I'm bored, bored, bored! I was right about Jason. He avoids me like I have the plague. I can't wait for school to start. It'll be something to do. Sure wish we lived closer to each other. I really miss you, Dawn . . .

The idea began to form in Dawn's head even before she finished reading Sandy's letter . . . camp. If Sandy could go, it might not be such a bad idea. If Sandy could go, it would be a fun thing to do, a fun place to go. But ONLY if Sandy could go.

She took the information and her idea to her parents that night at supper. "Do you really want to do this?" her dad asked.

Dawn nodded. "I think it might be fun, if Sandy's there."

Her mom hedged. "I don't know . . . You just got home . . . And what about your medications and tests?"

"I've been home for *ages*," Dawn defended. "At camp, I'll be around all the doctors and nurses. It's for kids with cancer. Of course, they'll take good care of us!" Suddenly, she wanted to go very much. She wanted to be around other kids like herself. But most of all, she wanted to see Sandy, her best friend.

"All right," her dad told her with a firm shake of his head. "If you want to go, I'll make the arrangements!"

81

CHAPTER
9

The camp matched the pictures in the brochure perfectly. The place was neat, clean and modern. There was a main complex of buildings with tree-lined trails and footpaths to cabins, stables, an Olympic-sized swimming pool and a magnificent blue lake.

The woods were beautiful, bright and green, cool and heavy with the scents of summer. Dawn fell in love with the peacefulness and the tranquility of the camp at once. She nervously checked in at the main building. She was eager to have her parents leave so that she could go exploring on her own. She was eager to try and track down Sandy.

"You're in Coyote cabin," a counselor sitting at a long table told her. "Here's a map. Just go outside and take the trail to the right, follow it past Fox and Eagle cabins and you'll be there." The counselor circled an area on Dawn's map and handed it to her.

Her dad picked up her bags and followed her out into the bright afternoon sun, down the winding leaf-strewn trail. They found Coyote cabin with ease. Dawn bounded up the concrete steps and entered the air-conditioned cabin. Eight neat bunks lined the walls. Each was headed by a dresser.

Her dad gave a low whistle. "Not bad. I'd say this place is as good as Holiday Inn," he said.

Dawn agreed, noticing that two of the beds had already been claimed. She staked out two, one for her and one for Sandy. "She's not here yet," Dawn said, her disappointment showing.

"She will be," her mom told her. "It's a long drive from West Virginia."

"She wouldn't be coming at all if Dr. Sinclair hadn't insisted," Dawn said. The camp was supposed to be for Ohio residents only. But Dr. Sinclair had requested that Sandy be allowed to attend.

"Yes," her dad mused. "Who's going to say 'No' to him?"

"There're at least fifty other kids coming," her mother informed Dawn. "Sandy's not the only friend you'll have."

"She's the only one I want right now," Dawn said. Unpacking her things, she took half a dresser, leaving the other half for her friend, and then she left the cabin to explore the grounds.

Together, with her family, Dawn wandered the trails. The paths were quiet, sun splashed with leaf patterns and shadows. Butterflies fluttered lazily in the air and tall trees towered overhead, reaching up, up into the clear sky. The sapphire blue lake was at the heart of the camp, stretching across to the horizon, mirror-calm and decorated with garlands of firs and pines.

By the time they arrived back at the central building, it was late afternoon and the spacious interior teemed with campers, their families and friends. Dawn searched the crowds for Sandy. Suddenly, a squeal from across the room caused her to spin.

Sandy hurtled across the floor shouting Dawn's name, and flung herself into Dawn's arms. Both girls jumped up and down, shouting, laughing and talking all at once. "I can't believe I'm here!" Sandy cried in her soft West Virginian accent.

"Me either!" Dawn shouted. "We're going to have so much fun! I've already saved us beds in our cabin!" Dawn told her.

They hopped around for a few more minutes, babbling with excitement. Finally, Dawn led Sandy outside toward Coyote cabin. Sandy's father struggled, red-faced with her luggage, trying to keep up.

"I just love it!" Sandy cried, after surveying the cabin.

Her father looked around, hesitant to leave her. "Now, Daddy, I'll be just fine," Sandy told him.

"You sure?" he asked. "It's just so far from home, Honey . . ."

Sandy rolled her eyes and led him back to the main building. Dawn's parents were still waiting amid the confusion of campers trying to check in. "Honestly, Pa! I want to be here. I'm gonna have a real good time. Now you get along, ya hear?" Sandy told him.

Reluctantly, the big man hugged his tiny daughter to him. Dawn hugged her parents good-bye, kissing them self-consciously, and watching as they left. Finally alone, she turned to Sandy and cried, "We're free!"

They renewed their friendship instantaneous-ly, as if no time had passed between them. They walked the trails, exploring the grounds and each other's lives.

"My hair's growing back," Dawn said, pulling off her scarf in the privacy of the woods.

"Mine, too," Sandy said. "And guess what? It's goin' to grow in curly. Can you believe it?" She pulled off her scarf, too, and each girl explored the thick growths of hair on the other's head.

They retied their scarfs and continued walking. "How's it goin' for you?" Sandy asked.

Dawn shrugged. "All right, I guess. I do exactly what the doctors tell me to do. I still do my Imaging every day. But sometimes I feel . . ." she groped for a word, " . . . old," she finished.

"I know what you mean," Sandy confided. "One day I was a kid and life's real simple. Then I got sick," she shrugged.

From far away, they heard the sound of a clanging bell. "What's that?" Sandy asked.

"That's the way they call you to meetings around here," she explained. "Come on, race you back to the main hall."

Both girls took off running and arrived back at the central building, breathless. Inside, clusters of campers were already seated on benches along the wall. Several counselors stood in the center of the room. Dawn recognized Joan Clarke and waved.

A young, dark-haired, muscular man, who looked like an athlete, blasted a whistle that stopped the noisy din of chatter and said, "I'm Dr. Ben Isaacson. Call me Ben. I'm in charge of this place and all of you. We have a few rules." A loud moan went up. Ben laughed and held up his hands. "But very few rules," he added.

Everybody clapped and cheered. "Many of you have been here before," he continued. "Some of you are new. You all have agenda sheets in your orientation packets. Right now, I want all of you to go back to your cabins, meet your counselors and plan to be back here at six o'clock sharp for dinner."

Another cheer went up. "Then we'll meet down by the lake at sunset for the official bonfire opening of the best little camp in the country!" Dr. Ben yelled. Kids clapped and cheered. Dawn caught their excitement. She scanned the room, seeing her fellow campers for the first time.

There were kids of every size and shape, some younger, several older than her. Many girls wore scarves. Several boys were bald and seemed proud of it. Some kids wore leg braces. A few were in wheel chairs. Others looked as healthy as horses with no trace of chemotherapy or radiation side effects.

"I'm gonna have a real good time," Sandy drawled in her ear. Dawn followed her gaze and saw two very good-looking boys on the far side of the room. Both were tall and lean. But before she could get a better look, the crowd broke up and everyone headed for their cabins and the adventure of the evening ahead.

* * * * *

The campers gathered down by the lake in time to watch the sun set. The brilliant red sphere balanced on the rim of the water like a beach ball. Then it slipped beyond the horizon, leaving the soft haze of twilight behind it.

Dawn and Sandy nestled on log benches facing a massive pyramid of twigs and logs. Excited whispers heralded the coming of the lighting of the bonfire. Dawn waited with anticipation. She looked out across the water in time to see a canoe slicing through the dark, glassy surface. Two people, dressed as Indians, dipped oars into the water, propelling the slender canoe toward their shore.

Dr. Ben stood and said in hushed tones, "The Indians were the first to see this land, the first to travel across this lake, the first to hunt this area. We pay tribute to them and their spirit of harmony with Nature."

By now, the Indians had landed their canoe on the shore. A man and a woman, dressed in the buckskin and feathers of an ancient Ohio tribe, emerged from the craft and walked to the side of the pile of wood.

Dr. Ben continued. "As you know, our ritual is the same every year. Soon we will light the bonfire. We'll gather before it, sing, roast marshmallows and watch the fire burn low. Once it's cooled, each of you will gather some of the ashes in a box and take them home with you. Guard them.

"Next year, when you return, you'll bring the ashes back and toss them onto that year's bonfire. In this way, each of us comes back to this place, bringing some of the past, leaving with some of the future. Will those of you who have ashes from last year please bring them forward?" he asked.

Over half of the kids stood up pulling small matchboxes from their pockets. Solemnly, they filed forward, opened their boxes and sprinkled the contents on the heap of wood. Some carried two boxes. One boy, who shook out the contents of two separate boxes said, "This is for Parker

Johnson, who died last January."

A girl shook out two boxes and said, "This is for Ruth Myers. She passed away in May."

Goose bumps traveled the length of Dawn's back. " 'Ashes to ashes, Dust to dust.' " She remembered the quote from Sunday School.

After all the ashes had been sprinkled, the Indians stepped forward and lit a torch. With a cry and a whoop, the man dipped the torch onto the wood, trotting around the pyramid, lighting it in several places. The dry twigs caught and the fire spread in bright consuming flames to the crest of the pile.

It burned and crackled and a giant cheer went up from the assembly. Dawn felt a dampness in her eyes for all the kids she'd never met who'd been here before her. Then she clapped and cheered, too. "I'll be back!" she told herself as she watched the great fire burn and glow in the darkening sky. "I promise. I'll be back!"

CHAPTER
10

"Don't look now, but those two boys are starin' at us," Sandy's soft whisper said in Dawn's ear. Dawn focused extra attention on the end of her marshmallow roasting stick. She slid her eyes casually to the direction Sandy had indicated.

Two guys, the same two she'd noticed earlier at the orientation, were indeed staring at her and Sandy! Dawn's heart did a staccato beat and she forced her attention back onto the marshmallow over the bonfire. It had turned charcoal black.

"It's ruined!" she moaned, tossing the gooey mess onto the ground.

Sandy giggled. "They're real cute, aren't they?"

"The marshmallows?" Dawn asked teasingly. But she agreed with her friend. Both boys were tall, well-built and very cute! One boy wore jeans. The other boy wore shorts showing lean, muscular, athletic legs. The one with jeans had a full head of curly brown hair, while the other boy's hair danced with bright blond glints from the firelight. Both looked vital and healthy.

The bonfire glowed lower and lower. The counselors led the group in some songs and Dawn kept noticing the way the two boys kept looking at her and Sandy. It made her feel feminine and exciting. The boys were definitely interested! It was a good feeling.

Dr. Ben, as the campers called him, stood up and raked sand over the dying embers of the fire, letting the night air cool and extinguish it. Other counselors handed out boxes and each camper quietly filed forward and received a small pile of the ashes from Dr. Ben.

Dawn closed her matchbox over its ashes and clutched it firmly in her hand. Afterward, Dr. Ben dismissed everyone to the cabins with the message, "Tomorrow's a big day. Breakfast is at eight A.M., followed by arts and crafts, swimming, lunch, rest, horseback riding, dinner, a nature walk and games in the mess hall. I suggest we all get some sleep!"

Cat calls and cries of "Boo!" filled the evening air. Dr. Ben laughed and held up his hands for silence. "All right! All right! But remember, we old people need our rest. After all, we're in training for the Special Olympics on the last day of camp. And we'll trounce the wimps who don't get their rest!"

More boos and hisses arose. Open challenges were loudly issued. And then everyone broke up and headed down the moonlit paths toward their cabins.

"What's the Special Olympics?" Sandy asked. Dawn shrugged, but it sounded like fun.

"It's a day of games and trophies," a male voice explained from behind them.

Both girls turned, and the two boys who'd been eyeing them all evening fell into step beside them. Dawn's mouth went dry. The boy next to her stood almost six feet. His muscular build rippled under his T-shirt and shorts. "Hi," he said. "I'm Greg Buchannan. This is my friend, Mike McConnell."

Dawn managed to utter her name. Sandy introduced herself as well.

"You talk funny," Mike blurted out at Sandy. "Where are you from?"

"West Virginia," Sandy drawled in her thickest accent. Dawn suppressed a giggle.

"Greg and I, we're from Cleveland," Mike said.

Greg asked Dawn, "This is your first year here, isn't it?"

"Yes," she said. "How about you?"

"We're veterans," Greg told her. "This is my third year and Mike's second."

Surprised, Dawn blurted, "You both have cancer?" She felt her cheeks flame and was glad it was dark. *Of course they have cancer, stupid!* she admonished herself.

"I've been in remission three years," Greg

said. "I like coming to camp. I look forward to it all year."

Three years! Both boys looked about 15 years old to Dawn. And they looked so strong and healthy.

"Which cabin are you in?" Greg asked Dawn. The moon ducked behind a cloud cover and the woods grew dark. Dawn pulled closer to the big blond boy next to her.

"Coyote," she said. "We're in Coyote cabin. How about you?"

"Quail," Greg said. Dawn noticed that Mike had fallen behind with Sandy. She was walking alone in the beautiful soft summer night with Greg. The hushed air of the woods filled with the scent of pine. Her heart thudded expectantly.

"You're going to have a great time," he said. They turned a corner on the trail and Coyote cabin rose out of the dark.

"Here we are," he stated.

Sandy and Mike arrived beside them. "See ya tomorrow at breakfast," Greg said, looking down at Dawn from his height. The moon reemerged and cast silver patterns on his hair and eyelashes.

"Sure," Dawn said, hoping she didn't sound too eager. "See you at breakfast."

Quickly, she and Sandy bounded into the cabin. The other girls had already arrived. Dawn let out her breath and felt a grin stretching from ear to ear.

Sandy squealed and plopped dramatically onto her bed. "I think I'm in love!" she sighed.

Dawn's heart swelled and she fell onto her bed in total contentment. "I'm going to have a wonderful time, Sandy. I just know it! Isn't Greg the cutest thing to ever breathe air?" she asked.

Both girls barely noticed their cabinmates as they settled in for the night. Dawn lay on her bunk in the dark for a long time, too excited to sleep. Whispers and giggles sounded throughout the cabin late into the night as girls swapped stories and told jokes. This was going to be the best two weeks of her life!

*　*　*　*　*

Greg and Mike sat with Dawn and Sandy at breakfast. The food tasted wonderful! Arts and crafts proved a little boring, so Mike livened things up by draping toilet paper over the natural beam rafters of the building's interior.

"Decoration!" he told everyone.

Before lunch, Sandy and Dawn eagerly changed into their swimsuits in their cabin, anxious to meet Greg and Mike by the pool. Joan surveyed her cabin charges and told the group of eight girls, "Ladies, do yourself a favor. If any of you are growing back hair from chemotherapy, please wear a scarf to the pool. It's no fun rubbing lotion on sunburned heads in the middle of the night!"

Everyone laughed, and Sandy and Dawn both retied their scarves securely.

At the pool, the aqua water beckoned invitingly. "Wish I wasn't still so skinny," Sandy complained, searching the crowd for Mike. "I don't have a curve left!"

Dawn agreed, wishing the same thing for herself. But the effects of the chemotherapy had almost worn off. Except for regrowing hair and adding about twelve pounds, she felt she looked pretty good in her one-piece emerald green swimsuit.

Greg and Mike arrived at the pool minutes after Dawn and Sandy. Greg was tanned and lean, testifying to many hours spent in the sun. Mike still wore jeans, but his bare chest was also firm and muscular like Greg's.

"You're not swimmin'?" Sandy asked, the disappointment showing in her voice.

Mike dropped his eyes and jammed his hands into the back pockets of his jeans. "Naw," he said.

"But why?" she asked, her blue eyes wide. "Can't you swim?"

Mike stood self-consciously for a moment. "I, uh, had a kind of bone cancer," he said quietly. "They had to cut off my left leg below the knee. I wear a prosthesis," he continued with a shrug, "you know, ... an artificial leg. I, uh, I have to take it off to go in the water."

The hot sun beat down. The sounds of kids

laughing and splashing enveloped the poolside air. The biting smell of chlorine filled Sandy's nose. Her insides ached for Mike.

Sandy looked him full in the face, tipped her head and said, "I don't care about your leg, Mike. I'd like you to come swimmin' with me."

Mike allowed his eyes to settle into hers. "What *does* bother me," Sandy continued, a teasing tone coming into her lilting voice, "is bein' around a boy who has more hair than I."

A slow, shy grin spread over Mike's face, reaching from his mouth to his eyes. He nodded and said, "You're all right, Sandy. You're all right."

The tension eased. Mike laughed and headed to his cabin to change. Sandy waited for him, and Dawn and Greg slid into the cool, fresh water.

"Actually," Greg said, breaking the surface and slinging the water off his face and hair, "Mike's a super swimmer. We're both on our high school swim team and we belong to the same swim club. We used to go to meets together all the time. Course, Mike can't compete any more. It's not a sport for a one-legged athlete. But he still works out and stays in shape."

"You're a swimmer?" Dawn asked, surprised.

"Since I was six," he told her. "I'm hoping for an athletic scholarship to college. I've already won meets and tournaments at the State and National levels. And who knows? Maybe I'll make it to the Olympics someday."

Dawn felt awed pleasure in his presence. Greg was planning a full and active future. And he had cancer, just like her. "What kind of cancer do you have?" she asked, no longer shy around him.

"Leukemia," he said, "since I was twelve. Two more years and they'll call me 'cured.' I think I'm going to make it." His blue eyes danced bright and colorful as the water. Small droplets clung to his golden skin and wet hair.

"Race you across the pool!" he called.

Dawn ducked under the water. She pushed off from the side of the pool in one smooth motion. She surfaced and stroked quickly over the surface.

"Hey!" Greg cried, caught by surprise.

Dawn laughed as he pulled alongside her with only a few strokes. Then he slowed and glided next to her through the water to the far side. She'd never felt happier, never more joyful.

"You're not a bad swimmer!" Greg said as they touched the far wall.

"Thanks," Dawn said. "I love sports."

Just then Sandy and Mike swam up alongside them. Dawn couldn't help but glance below the rippling water at Mike. His thick and muscular thigh ended at his knee. But he pushed off from the wall with his good leg and did a beautiful back flip under the water. Sandy clapped gleefully as he surfaced and Mike took her hand and pulled her playfully up to his chest.

Greg tapped Dawn on the shoulder. She

glided toward him in the water and his strong hands reached out for her. She realized, suddenly, that camp was only two weeks long. There would be only two weeks with Greg, Sandy, and Mike, only two weeks out of an entire year . . .

CHAPTER
11

Glorious summer days passed in idyllic splendor. The four campers went swimming, riding, canoeing and on nature hikes. They spent velvet summer nights at barbecues, camp movies and on long moonlight walks. Greg Buchannan became friend, beau and big brother to Dawn. Mike became the same to Sandy.

They sat under the trees together after lunch and during the heat of the day, relaxing, talking, sharing. They talked about having cancer. There was a bond between them, an invisible thread that bound them together for all their tomorrows.

"I'm a lot more serious about my future," Mike confessed one day. "Sometimes the guys I hang around with seem to waste so much of their time and energy on the dumbest things!"

Sandy laughed and nodded. "Isn't it the truth? I have friends who think a Saturday night without a phone call or a date is grounds for suicide," she said.

Dawn agreed. "I wonder a lot about going back to school. Will my old friends treat me normally?" she asked.

Greg shrugged. "Some will. Some won't. Sometimes you have to start all over again. You have to prove to them that you're all right, you know, socially acceptable. People are still afraid of cancer. One of my friends kept away from me because he thought he'd catch cancer if he was around me!" he said.

The other three broke out laughing at the idea. "What a dumbo!" Dawn cried.

The hot afternoon sun beat down through the canopy of the overhead trees. Sunlight and shadows flitted across Greg's face and shoulders. Dawn watched as he chewed on a long stem of grass. It was so easy to be around him. He *understood*. He really understood all the things she was feeling, because he had felt them, too. Would any other boy ever understand? Would the boys back home in her circle of friends understand and accept her the way Greg did?

"Hey!" Mike cried suddenly, sitting up from his prone position on the grass. "Not to change the subject, but I have a dynamite idea!"

His friends leaned in eagerly. "What?" "Tell us!" they whispered, catching the excitement in his voice.

"Let's 'get' Dr. Ben!" he grinned.

"How'd you mean?" Sandy asked.

"You know," Mike said, his brown eyes

twinkling. "Let's play a trick on him, something funny. Let's make it something he'll remember every year he comes to this camp!"

Sandy squealed mischievously. "Let's!" she said.

"What do you have in mind?" Greg asked, his blue eyes lighting up at the thought.

"How about a midnight raid with water balloons?" Dawn suggested. "Imagine being 'bombed' at midnight out of a sound sleep with a blast from a water balloon!"

Mike's eyes sparkled. "That's not bad, Dawn. What else?" he asked.

"Well," Sandy drawled. "Once, to get even with one of my brothers, I stole his underwear and sewed flowers all over them. It took him days to pick all the threads off. He was the talk of his gym class for weeks!" she laughed.

"We'll run them up the flagpole!" Greg shouted. "Can you picture the look on everybody's face when we go to breakfast and see Dr. Ben's underwear flying from the flagpole!"

The four of them dissolved into helpless laughter, then set about making their plans. "After we hit him with water balloons," Mike said, "he won't be expecting anything else. I'll get the underwear while the place is in confusion."

They decided to make the "hit" the next night. "Once everybody's asleep, Greg and I'll come to Coyote cabin and get you two," Mike said.

"We'll tap on the window, lightly. Then you two sneak out, and we'll go over to Dr. Ben's cabin. Greg and I'll sneak in it. You two pass us the balloons through the window. We'll make the hit, get the merchandise and then split."

"Sounds good to me," Sandy said. Dawn clapped with anticipation.

"I heard he sleeps with a rope surrounding his bed. The floor is covered with pots and pans," Greg offered. "That's so no one can get near his bed."

Mike snapped his fingers to dismiss the obstacle. "No problem," he said. "We'll be so sneaky, he'll never know what hit him!"

At arts and crafts the next morning, each of them took a handful of balloons from the craft supplies. That afternoon, they carefully filled them with water. Then Dawn and Sandy put them inside their shower caps and stashed them under their bunks.

"My poor cap looks like it's about to have a litter of kittens," Sandy remarked slyly to Mike at supper.

"Sh—sh!" he cautioned. "Doc Ben has spies all over the place."

As if to underscore Mike's warning, that night after a movie Dr. Ben stood up and said, "It has been brought to my attention that a lot of balloons have mysteriously 'disappeared' from the craft supplies."

An excited buzz swept around the campers.

Dawn felt her color darken. But she [...] facade of complete surprise.

Dr. Ben held up his hands and co[...] know that there are campers here who th[...] are smarter and more clever than us counselor[...] he started. A murmur of protest sounded in the room.

"However," he cried, his dark eyes teasing with challenge. "There's not a camper been born who can outwit, outsmart or outdo Dr. Ben Isaacson!"

The protest grew to open hisses and verbal challenges. Mike and Greg looked especially innocent during Dr. Ben's speech. But when the meeting broke up and everyone was dismissed, Greg leaned down to Dawn and whispered, "Tonight! We hit tonight. Tell Sandy. We'll come for you at midnight!"

With total anticipation, Dawn and Sandy went to their cabin and prepared for bed. They slipped on their nightgowns over their clothes. They crawled into bed and, once the lights went out, feigned sleep. It seemed like hours before Dawn recognized the calm, even breathing of deep sleep from her cabinmates.

Dawn heard the noise first. It sounded like little scratches on their window. She reached over and poked Sandy. "I hear the signal," she whispered. Dawn's heart pounded with the tingle of the upcoming adventure.

Cautiously, they crept out of bed and slipped

to the window. Sandy slowly slid the window up and leaned out. Mike rose from the bushes to greet her.

"Got the bombs?" he asked.

Dawn dropped to her knees and slid the bulging shower caps out from under her bed. She handed one to Sandy who passed it out the window to Greg and Mike. Next, Dawn swung her legs out the window and felt Greg's strong hands grab her waist. In another minute, Sandy boosted herself onto the windowsill, and Greg hauled her down to the bushes, too. There, the four of them hovered for a moment, breathing hard, quieting their nerves.

"Let's go!" Mike ordered.

They crouched and stealthily crept through the woods toward Lion cabin, where Dr. Ben and his male staff slept.

"This is going to be a piece of cake!" Mike whispered. "Now, here's what I want Sandy and Dawn to do. Greg is going to get in through the window. Then he'll help me inside. You two keep a lookout and pass us the bombs. Once the battle starts, look for me to toss out the underwear. Once you get it, take off! Go back to your cabin. Get in bed and don't look back."

"But what about you guys?" Sandy asked.

"We'll split. Don't worry," Mike said. "But it's important that Doc Ben thinks that the water balloons were the object of the raid. We can't let him suspect there's anything else going on.

Okay? Is everything ready?"

Dawn nodded and squeezed Greg's hand in the dark. Quickly, he leaned forward and brushed her mouth with his. "For luck!" he said. Her heart pounded with flushed surprise.

Greg raised the window and struggled to haul himself up over the ledge. He disappeared inside, then leaned out and reached down for Mike. In moments, both had vanished into the hushed darkness of the cabin. A minute later, Greg leaned out and Sandy and Dawn passed them the water balloons.

The girls crouched in the dark bushes, clutching each other's hand and suppressing adrenalin-soaked giggles. Suddenly, the cabin erupted with shouts, cries and yells. "What the?" "Hey! What's happening?"

"Bonsai!" Mike yelled. Splat after splat could be heard. Confusion and mayhem reined. Dawn wished she could see inside the cabin, but she and Sandy crouched against the outside wall, awaiting their prize to sail through the window.

Minutes later, an object was flung out the open window. Dawn scooped it up and stuffed it in her top. Then she and Sandy took off running. They never looked behind them and arrived back at their cabin winded and delirious with success.

"We made it!" Sandy whispered from the ground below their window.

"Not yet!" Dawn warned. She gathered her strength and grabbed the outside of the windowsill. Then she hauled herself up over the ledge. She was grateful for her sports background. Her arms were still strong and she got inside noiselessly. She reached out to Sandy, and her friend scrambled in after her.

Quickly they climbed into their beds. Dawn lay perfectly still, her ears straining for any signs that they'd been heard. All was quiet. Under her covers, she pulled the lump of material out of her top. Even in the dark she could tell that it was a pair of men's underwear. They'd done it! The four of them together had pulled off the ultimate prank.

She hoped Mike and Greg had gotten away. Sandy took the pants and sneaked into the bathroom. There she sat for over an hour on the floor with her small sewing kit. Dawn checked on her and found Sandy's handiwork perfect. The underwear was adorned with bright embroidered flowers, butterflies and bees.

Dawn took a laundry marker and scrawled across the seat: "The Fearless Four!" Finally, Sandy folded them up and stuck them under her pillow.

Dawn slept fitfully. But early the next morning, when the rest of the cabin was just awakening, she and Sandy excused themselves for an early walk to the mess hall. They walked swiftly toward their destination, the empty flagpole.

The dew clung to the woods and the fresh

smell of morning filled the hazy air. Dawn's pulse raced with anticipation. At the flagpole they paused, looked around for privacy, clipped the newly decorated underwear on the flag hooks, and hauled it up the chain. A slight morning breeze caught the new "flag" and the girls watched as the brightly emblazoned pants fluttered and flapped at the top of the pole.

They swiftly slipped into the mess hall where Greg and Mike sat in wide-eyed innocence waiting for them. "You made it!" Sandy cried with delight.

"He never knew what hit him!" Greg whispered.

They all stifled laughs and waited for the hungry campers and counselors to descend on the mess hall and see the result of their night's work. Beneath the table, Greg took Dawn's hand. He held it tightly and her heart danced.

From outside, they began to hear excited cries, waves of laughter and gasps of shock and surprise as groups arrived for breakfast. They arose and walked casually outside, blending into the crowds that stood gazing and pointing up at the top of the flagpole.

"Look at that!" a boy yelled.

"Do we salute?" someone else asked.

"Hey, Doc Ben!" a counselor called. The bewildered doctor stood at the base of the pole, scratching his head and looking up at his underwear fluttering in the breeze. "I thought you were too smart for these kids!"

The entire camp broke out into wolf whistles, shouts and excited chatter. The red-faced Dr. Ben shrugged his shoulders, scanned the faces of his charges and shrugged. "I'll get even at the Special Olympics!" he called. Then he burst out laughing and saluted the flowered underwear high overhead in the morning sun.

CHAPTER
12

The camp talked about the "Fearless Four" for days while gearing up for the final days and the long awaited Special Olympics. Dawn was eager for the promised day of fun. But she was dreading it, too. The Special Olympics meant the end of camp, the end of summer and the end of the best time she'd ever had in her life.

Dr. Ben divided the sixty campers and twelve counselors into six teams of twelve. He passed out sheets of paper outlining the events and the rules. Every team held strategy and planning meetings to discuss winning the overall trophy. Dawn found herself on the same team as Greg. Sandy and Mike were assigned another team.

The night before the big sports event, a band arrived at the recreation hall and set up for dancing and entertainment. The night was hot and muggy. Dawn dressed in crisp white shorts and a sleeveless green top and sandals and met Greg inside the screened Rec room.

Sandy, dressed in pink, met Mike. The four of them watched while the band warmed up and then played the top songs of summer. Pedro Mendez performed a break dancing routine that caused everyone to howl with delight. Dawn stood and watched, feeling Greg's presence behind her. His hands rested casually on her shoulders and her heart swelled with pleasure and happiness.

Later they danced slowly in one another's arms. Her head didn't even reach his shoulder. "Let's go for a walk," he said in her ear. She agreed, and together they left the dance and went into the cooling night air.

Greg took her hand and they walked silently down the moonlit footpath toward the lake. Dawn felt contentment and peace settle within her. They reached the edge of the water and stood watching as it lapped gently against the expanse of white sand along its shore. The moon cut a long white beam across the dark surface of the water. From far away she heard frogs and crickets.

"Look!" Dawn said. And she pointed up at blinking fireflies in the sky above them.

Greg took both her hands in his and pulled her against his broad chest. Her mouth went dry and her blood pounded in her ears. "Let's write," he said, his voice husky sounding.

Dawn's spirits soared. "I'd like that," she said.

"And we'll meet here again next summer," he urged.

"Next summer," she echoed. She looked up at him. The moon struck his face from the side, lighting it in pearly silver hues. Dawn rose on her tiptoes, held her breath and closed her eyes. He kissed her tenderly.

Fireflies and stars twinkled around them. The moon glimmered, shooting off sparks of silver into the blackness of the night. Dawn would remember this night for the rest of her life.

* * * * *

The day of the Special Olympics was hot and humid. But the teams were ready. "The first event," Dr. Ben announced over the PA system. "The first event will be the Oatmeal Pass!"

Eagerly, each team lined up in rows. Each member sat behind another, single file on the ground in a line of six. Dawn's team, the Bandits, snuggled close behind one another's back waiting for the starter's gun to sound.

The lead man, Dusty Willis, sat with his arms outstretched. He was ready to receive the glob of cooked oatmeal into his cupped hands that rested in Joan Clarke's ladle.

"Now remember!" Dr. Ben said. "You must pass the oatmeal over your head to the person directly behind you. It must pass over your heads! The team to reach the end of the line first with the most amount of oatmeal remaining, wins! Ready?"

He fired his starter's pistol and the Great Oatmeal Race was on! Joan shook off the cold, wet glob of oatmeal into Dusty's hands who lifted the soggy mess over his head to the outstretched hands behind him. The new hands received it. They passed to Dawn and as it slid and slithered into her hands, she jerked it high above her head to Greg, sitting behind her. A large wet blob of it slid between her fingers and squished onto her head.

Dawn squealed with shivery tingles and dumped the mess into Greg's hands, laughing and yelling. The diminishing ladle of oatmeal passed swiftly from team member to team member, each trying to keep the slippery mess from oozing out of his hands. At the back of the line, Joan stood urging them on and holding the ladle to receive what was left.

The oatmeal arrived in record time. With a shout, the Bandits stood up celebrating their victory. Dawn laughed at Greg who had oatmeal plastered across his chest. Her own upper arms and head also felt gooey with the mess. "We won!" Greg cried, and the entire team cheered.

From there, the teams moved over to the Egg Toss competition. Partners lined up and started tossing a raw egg between them. After each toss they took a giant step backward, until the couple from each team who kept their egg unbroken the longest, won the event.

Dawn and Greg paired off and began tossing

the fragile egg. Dawn caught it beautifully and tossed it back. Greg caught it perfectly. A screech beside her told Dawn that Sandy hadn't been as fortunate. Her egg had broken in her hands.

Over and over Dawn and Greg tossed their egg. Over and over they caught it without mishap. All but four pairs were eliminated from the competition. Dawn concentrated hard and tossed the egg high in the air. Greg moved beneath it, his arms raised to receive it and cushion its landing. Disaster struck. The egg hit too hard and disintegrated in his hands.

"Ugh!" he cried as the yellow runny mess slithered in thick drops through his fingers. Dawn collapsed into helpless laughter and he threatened to wipe his hands on her shirt.

"Don't you dare, Greg Buchannan!" Dawn shrieked and took off running.

Next, the teams passed oranges from neck to neck down their line. Without using hands, the feat proved quite difficult, but after the Bandits completed this round they were in first place.

"We're not defeated yet!" Mike called, rallying his team to win the Water Balloon Toss event.

The Bandits took the Three-Legged Race and Mike's team took the Sack Hop. The other teams, now far behind, began to take sides and cheer for either the Bandits or the Scorpions.

"It looks as if we need a tie breaker!" Dr. Ben

called after totaling up the scores.

The teams cheered. "I suggest the Flour-Candy Hunt!" Dr. Ben announced. Dawn didn't know what it was, but it sounded like fun. Counselors brought out twelve paper plates heaped with white flour and set the plates on the picnic tables under a pavilion.

"Now!" Dr. Ben said. "Believe it or not, there is a piece of candy buried in each mound of flour. You contestants have to find it."

That seems too simple, Dawn thought.

". . . without using your hands!" Dr. Ben finished. The contestants groaned. "It's kind of like bobbing for apples!" he said. "Dig through that flour with your face! Scratch around in that white fluff with your nose and find that sucker!" Dr. Ben yelled.

He blasted a whistle and the contestants lunged forward with their faces. Dawn felt the flour clinging to her mouth and nose. It stuck in her nostrils and clung heavily to her eyelashes. Her nose bumped something solid. The candy! She groveled for it all the harder, sending flour up around her head in white puffs.

Suddenly, a shout went up. Dawn picked up her head in time to see Sandy standing, grinning a white-faced smile of triumph, with a cellophane-wrapped hard candy dangling between her teeth. A shout of victory went up and Mike picked her up, whirled her around in the air, and proclaimed the Scorpions the "Victors."

116

The Special Olympic games ended after a wiener roast and a watermelon pig-out. Trophies went to every team and then all the campers and staff marched down to the lake for a giant bonfire as the sun set over the water.

As Dawn sat close to Greg and watched the flames of the final bonfire burn low, a large lump rose in her throat. "I'm going to miss everybody so much," she said in a whisper. Her voice cracked slightly and Greg hugged her shoulders to him.

"Yeah, you will," he confirmed. "But you'll get busy again. School will start and soon it's Christmas, then spring. Then before you know it," he snapped his fingers, "summer's back!"

A dark thought crossed her mind. "D-Do you think we'll all be here next year?" she asked, scanning the faces that had grown so familiar to her during the last two weeks.

"Most of us will," Greg said. "But not everyone. . . "

Dawn didn't ask any more. She couldn't bear to think of one of them not being here the next year. Yet, every kid around the bonfire had a form of cancer. Every camper in the group had his own particular battle to go home and fight, including herself.

Dawn leaned against Greg's chest and he brushed the side of her cheek with his fingers. She sighed, wishing she could preserve this moment forever under glass. But she couldn't.

Tomorrow she would go home. Tomorrow she'd go back to blood tests, bone marrow aspirations and clinic visits. Tomorrow her life would pick up where she'd left it, two weeks before.

CHAPTER
13

Once Dawn returned home, melancholy settled over her. She missed camp. She missed Sandy, Greg, and Mike. She missed the carefree days. She was lonely and sad. Sensing her mood, her mom involved Dawn as quickly as possible with preparations for returning to school. They spent three days shopping and reorganizing Dawn's wardrobe. They went to lunch together. They drove to distant towns and shopping malls, " . . . for a better selection," Mrs. Rochelle told her daughter.

Dawn also returned to the clinic at the hospital and endured the testing for signs that her cancer was still dormant. The tests were fine. She was still in remission.

Dawn saw her friends. She prepared to return to school with them. She visited with the principal and spoke with the counselor. Her work had always been above average. It was decided that she could go into the eighth grade. And Mrs. Talbert said her position was still open on the cheerleading squad.

School started without fanfare. Dawn thought she'd be more excited. But she wasn't. Her classes were standard. The only excitement came when she arrived at her history room and saw that Jake Macka was in the same class.

"Odd," she told herself. It was odd that her heart should still pound with excitement every time she saw him, even after the wonderful summer weeks with Greg, even after the kiss Greg had given her . . . even after the letter he'd written her. It was still Jake Macka who made her pulse race, her palms perspire and her mouth go dry.

Sometimes at school she felt like a freak. The kids who knew her were friendly. Those who didn't know her whispered about her behind her back. Once, when she went into the girls' restroom, the conversation stopped cold. She quickly washed her hands and left, her cheeks burning. "Dawn Rochelle . . . " they whispered. "You know, the girl with cancer . . . ."

Dawn had been in classes three weeks, when a letter arrived from Sandy. Eagerly, she tore it open in the privacy of her bedroom. Fear mounted within her as she read it.

Dear Dawn,
Bad news! I've had a relapse. I'm no longer in remission. I started feeling bad again right after I got home from camp. I didn't tell my folks right away. But soon I

had to tell them. The tests showed that the leukemia was active again.

Oh, Dawn! I'm so depressed. I can't face the thought of going through all that chemotherapy again. But as bad as I feel, it isn't half as hard on me as on my folks. You should see my poor daddy! He's a basket case. He's talked to Dr. Sinclair a couple of times, and Dr. Sinclair wants us to come back to Columbus right away. He says that we might have to think about a bone marrow transplant. Boy! Did that set my daddy off!

Now he's talking about taking me to some clinic in Mexico. I truly hope he changes his mind. I don't want to go to Mexico! As bad as the chemotherapy is, I'd rather be with Dr. Sinclair. Besides, you could come visit me if I was in Columbus!

On a brighter side, Mike wrote me. I sure miss camp. And I sure miss him, too. He sent me his picture and I sent him mine. I never liked a boy more than Mike. I can't wait until next summer when I can see him again at camp.

I'd better close now. I'm feeling kind of tired and weak. Please write soon. How's

school going? Do you hear from Greg? I
wish I could go back to school.

                                    Love,
                                    Sandy

Dawn quickly sat down and wrote Sandy a
letter filled with dismay, sympathy and hopeful-
ness that things would change for her very soon.
Then Dawn showed both letters to her mother.
"I'm sorry, Honey..." was all her mom could say.
Somehow Dawn knew that in her mother's
thought was, "Thank God it's not YOU."

                *   *   *   *   *

"Did you see how Jake ran in for that
touchdown?" Rhonda cried to her friends over
the table in the Video Shak. Dawn took a long sip
from the straw in her glass and listened to the
excited babble of the girls surrounding her.
    Yes, she had seen how Jake had run into the
end zone for the winning touchdown. The whole
school had seen it. The fans had cheered. The
coach had done a cartwheel. The cheerleaders
had gone crazy with joy. The whole school had
turned out for the rivalry match between Adams
and Harrison. Jake Macka was the hero of the
day. He'd been carried off the field on his
teammates' shoulders.
    Dawn had cheered for him, too. She cheered

for him so loudly that she'd almost lost her voice. He'd glanced at her, just for a moment, his dark brown eyes sparkling with the excitement of his accomplishment. Her heart had thudded, crazily. Then he'd turned away, basking in the glory of his heroic moment.

At home, that afternoon, there was another letter from Sandy.

Dear Dawn,

As you can tell by the postmark, I'm writing you from Mexico. *Olé*! I was real scared at first. But my daddy is sure he's doing the right thing. Not even Mama could talk him out of bringing me down here. And you know how persuasive my mama can be!

My doctor is Dr. Sanchez. He's a nice little man with a moustache. His accent is soft and cute. I think his clinic is real nice, too. It's light and airy with red tiles and murals all over the place. There's a real nice garden with fountains, cactus and strange looking trees. I can see the mountains from the window in my room. They're all purple and hazy, real different from the Alleghenys.

There's no chemotherapy either, just lots of fresh food, vitamins and sunshine. I declare, here it is nearly October and

it's hotter than a West Virginia summer!
I'm tired a lot, but I don't hurt. And I
still have my hair! It's growing back real
nice with some curl. I figure that by
Christmas, I'll be able to use my combs
again.

You can write me here at the clinic in
Mexico City. Please write soon.

Love,
Sandy

P.S. I'm learning Spanish. *Mi amiga*
means "My friend."

*   *   *   *   *

The October air was crisp and brilliant on the
Saturday of the Adams Junior High Fall Carnival. Booths were set up throughout the halls of
the school and on the Physical Education field.
Dawn felt invigorated by the smell of the autumn
afternoon and the general excitement of the
day.
The trees were hung with the bright colors of
fall—red, gold and mottled shades of brown and
orange. A small midway attracted kids and
families to roller coaster and Ferris wheel rides.
Dawn took her turn in the cheerleaders' booth,
selling tickets for the baseball pitch. It was the
most popular booth at the Carnival.
The principal had agreed to sit above a tank of

water. A bull's-eye meant a dunk in the chilling water below. Ticket buyers got three tries. Dawn was doing landslide business and the money that the booth earned would go toward uniforms and traveling expenses.

"I'll take two dollars' worth," the boy's voice said.

Dawn looked up at Jake Macka. Her heart did its now familiar staccato beat. "Only two dollars?" she teased.

"Hey, I don't want to drown the man!" Jake countered.

Egged on by his friends, Jake scored four perfect pitches out of six. The shivering, water-soaked principal hauled himself out of the tank for the last time and held his hands up in a sign of surrender. "Mercy! Mercy!" he pleaded.

"You're ruining our business," Dawn told Jake with a chiding tone. "Now who's going to take his place?"

"Not me!" Jake said, backing off from the group that surrounded him.

"Why not?" Todd called. "Chicken?"

Good-natured jeers and cheers caused Jake to finally surrender. He stripped off his shirt and sneakers and crawled up onto the platform above the water tank. A flurry of ticket buying followed. Dawn watched, giggling each time the baseball struck its mark.

In a half-hour, Jake was thoroughly soaked and he, too, abandoned the platform. Dawn brought a towel to him.

He shivered. "T-Thanks," he said and wrapped the towel around his shoulders.

"Thank *you*," she told him. "You didn't have to do that. But it raised a lot of money for us. Thanks for doing it." She felt her cheeks flush slightly. Jake looked at her as if he might say something.

Self-consciously, Dawn reached up and touched her hair. It had grown longer and was fashioned in a cute pixy style, but she wished she had long hair right now. She knew Jake liked long hair.

"It was fun," Jake told her with a shrug. Then he left with a group of his friends.

One week later, she got another letter from Sandy.

Dear Dawn, (*Mi amiga*)

I sure enjoyed your last letter. It must be fun to be in school and all. I sure hope you and Jake become special friends. If you like him more than Greg, then he must be something special! Stop thinking so much about him being normal and you being sick. You're not sick! You're in remission. I'm sick!

Just teasing. But I have been feeling poorly more and more. Dr. Sanchez is very kind. He gives me lots of support and I'm not scared anymore of what might happen to me. At least I don't hurt all the time. That pleases my daddy 'cause he can't stand to see me hurting.

Sometimes I don't think I'm getting well. Sometimes I wish I was back with Dr. Sinclair. But I'm here and the days are so bright and sunny and nice. Say *Buenos dias* (Good day) to all your family for me. I'll sign this off with more Spanish that I've learned. *Buenos noches, mi amiga. Vaya con Dios*. It means: Good night, my friend. Go with God.

Love,
Sandy

*　*　*　*　*

The doorbell rang and Dawn called from the crest of the stairs, "I'll get it!" She bounded down the staircase from her bedroom and flung open the front door. A man in a uniform was standing on her porch.

"Telegram," he said, holding out a clipboard and a yellow envelope. Suddenly, Dawn's whole body began to shake. *Who would send us a telegram?* she wondered. She grew cold.

"Who is it?" her mom asked, walking to the open door from the kitchen. She wiped her hands on a dish towel and signed for the telegram. Grimly, she closed the door and stood looking at the envelope.

"Do you want me to open it?" she asked Dawn softly.

Dawn nodded, too numb to speak. Her heart hammered. The aroma of her mom's baking apple pie filled the house.

The air stood still. The sound of the grandfather clock kept its rhythm. Her mom's voice trembled as she read aloud:

"We lost our beloved Sandy yesterday, 10 A.M. Stop. She died peacefully — no pain. Stop. We're flying her home to West Virginia for burial. Stop. Package for Dawn to follow. Stop. The Chandlers."

CHAPTER
14

Somehow Dawn made it up the stairs to her bedroom. She never remembered going. She only remembered being there. She only remembered sitting on her bed and staring into space. She remembered feeling cold, so cold.

"Honey," her mother said, sitting next to her on her bed. "Dawn," she said as she touched her daughter's thin shoulder.

"She's gone. Oh, Mom, Sandy's really gone," Dawn cried.

"She'll never be gone, Honey," her mom said, "not as long as you remember her. She'll always live in your memory, in your heart."

Dawn turned her eyes, still bright and stinging with prickly tears, toward her mother. "It hurts, Mom," she whispered. "It hurts." She looked up at her bedroom wall. The poster was still there, the poster Sandy had drawn. Mr. Ruggers sat valiantly astride his big white horse. Beneath his hooves, piles of attacking green globs snapped and snarled.

"All that they did to me in the hospital . . . " Dawn continued quietly. "All the needles and tests and hurting . . . None of it hurt like this." The tears came then, a flood of tears. They were tears with big wracking sobs that shook her body, sobs from the core of her being, tears from the pit of her anguish.

Dawn's mom held her crying daughter. Dawn cried for all the times she'd never cried, for all the pain, for all the children, for Sandy, Mike, and Greg and for herself, too. She cried until she gagged, until she felt like she would turn inside out. She was so empty, void and spent that she couldn't move, and then she slept.

Dawn didn't go to school for two days. She lay red-eyed and silent, alone in her room. She ate. She took her medications. She did all the mechanical things that her parents made her do. When Dr. Sinclair called her, she knew that her parents had called him about her. She told him she'd be all right.

"Your tests are good, Dawn," he told her on the phone.

"I'm not worried about me," she told him. "I know I'm in remission and I plan to stay in remission. Really, it's okay."

Her friends called. But she didn't want to talk to any of them, yet. Some sent her cards in the mail. They all had known about her friend Sandy. They were all sorry. She got one mystery card. It had a picture of a Koala bear on the front with a bandage across his forehead. Inside it read: "I can't *bear* to see you hurt!" It was unsigned.

One week later the package came. Dawn opened it in her room alone with Mr. Ruggers looking down from his shelf. She tore off the paper and lifted the lid. A note rested on top. Mrs. Chandler's flowing scroll had written:

Dear Dawn,

These are the special items that Sandy asked us to forward to you. She cared about you very much, often calling you her very best friend. Please keep in touch with us. We want to know when you make that five year mark. Do it for Sandy.

The Chandlers

The first thing Dawn opened was the box of hair combs. She ran her fingers over all the brightly colored hair decorations and smiled inwardly. "I'll grow my hair long again," she said aloud.

Next, she lifted out a popcorn necklace. It looked slightly shriveled and the glitter flaked off in her hands. But it, too, caused her to smile. She remembered the day Sandy had made it.

She found the matchbox full of ashes from camp. A lump swelled in her throat. She'd put it with her own box and take them both to camp

131

with her next year. "I'll write Mike," she said into the stillness of her room, as if someone besides Mr. Ruggers would hear her.

She found Mike's picture in Sandy's diary, marking one special page. It was dated the last night of camp in August.

> *Mike kissed me tonight. How wonderful it was! I've never been kissed like that! Wow! 'Course only Dawn knows that I've only been kissed once before anyway! And she won't tell. I can't wait 'til next summer. Then Mike and I can practice some more . . . .*

The letters began to squiggle and squirm before Dawn's eyes. "I'll have to read this later," she said, sniffing hard against the threatening wave of nostalgic tears.

The last thing in the box was a page from the Bible. It had been torn out and marked up. But it was obvious that Sandy had read it many times.

Ecclesiastes 3:1-8

To every thing there is a season, and a time to every purpose under the heaven:

2 A time to be born, and a time to die; a time to plant, and a time to pluck up that which is planted;

3 A time to kill, and a time to heal; a time to break down, and a time to build up;

4 A time to weep, and a time to laugh; a time to mourn, and a time to dance;

5 A time to cast away stones, and a time to gather stones together; a time to embrace, and a time to refrain from embracing;
6 A time to get, and a time to lose; a time to keep, and a time to cast away;
7 A time to rend, and a time to sew; a time to keep silence, and a time to speak;
8 A time to love, and a time to hate; a time of war, and a time of peace.

Dawn pondered the page for a long while. It was true. Sandy's "season" was over. She'd gone home to God. The thought brought Dawn great comfort and made her more determined than ever to live her own "season" to its fullest. She shut the box and put it away on a shelf.

* * * * *

Cheerleading practice was over. Dawn slammed her locker shut and mopped her face with a tissue. It had been a hard workout.

"Want to go over to the Video Shak?" Jill asked. "Kathy, Rhonda, and I are going to get a soda. Boy! Am I whipped!"

"You go on ahead," Dawn told them, spinning the dial on her combination lock. "I'll catch up. I have a few things to do."

"All right," Jill said. "We'll meet you there. Hurry!"

Dawn watched the trio of chattering girls head off down the hall. She'd meet up with them later. She glanced down the deserted hall, lingering

133

casually, waiting for the football team to crash through the gym doors. Their practice was over. Jake might pass her way any minute.

Dawn clutched her books to her chest and tried to look preoccupied. But it was hard to do in an empty hall. She grew nervous. *He'll know you hung around waiting!* she chided herself. *Who do you think you're kidding, Rochelle?*

Finally, after a short internal war, she decided to try and catch her friends and quickly left the hallway. Outside, the blustery November wind blew cold and shivery in her face. She'd forgotten her sweater in her locker. "Great," she moaned privately.

Overhead, gray clouds scudded across the sky and bare tree branches scraped against each other. Dawn hurried, but she couldn't see her friends in the distance. Now she'd have to walk alone. *Waiting for Jake . . . dumb idea,* she chastised herself.

"Hey, Dawn! Wait up!" Jake's voice called to her. She stopped dead in her tracks and spun, her heart pounding. She managed a feeble smile, hoping that she looked more casual than she felt.

"Where're you going?" he asked. The wind blew his dark, freshly washed hair over his forehead. She wanted to reach up and flip it away with her fingers.

"To the Video Shak," she said.

"Me, too," he told her after a brief pause. "Can

I walk there with you?" He smiled.

She nodded, and he fell into step beside her. They scuffled along through the dead leaves in awkward silence.

"I-uh, I'm sorry about your friend," he said.

She shrugged. "A lot of kids are cured," she said, then felt stupid for saying it.

"Yeah," he said. "I did some reading about it." Dawn shivered. "You're cold!" he added. It was a statement, not a question.

"I forgot my sweater in my locker," she said.

He stopped, dropped his books to the ground and pulled off his jacket. He draped it over her shoulders. She snuggled against it. It was still warm from his body and smelled faintly of soap and shampoo. He laughed. "It's about four sizes too big," he said.

Her cheeks flushed. "Thanks," she said. "It's nice and warm."

Jake bent, scooped up his books and they resumed walking to the Video Shak. "It's the season," he said.

"What?" she asked, with a slight gasp.

"The season," he explained, startled by her response. "You know, the season for Thanksgiving, the season for Christmas, the season for snow." He laughed slightly and admitted, "I like the snow. I like ice skating and snowball fights, you know, dumb stuff."

Dawn smiled at him and nodded. "I like snow,

too," she said. "And you're right. It is the season."

Jake glanced at her and Dawn smiled shyly into his dark brown eyes. They walked on, alone in their private world as the weak November sun struggled out from behind a cloud bank and cast long shadows on the brown earth.

Its rays felt warm and soft and sweet.

To learn more about the different types of cancer and the symptoms in children and teenagers, contact your local chapter of the American Cancer Society.